T0114616

Of Life, Love and Death

Published by
Luviri Press
P/Bag 201 Luwinga
Mzuzu 2

ISBN   978-99960-66-77-1
    eISBN 978-99960-98-23-9

Luviri Reprints no. 13
First published by WASI in 2009

The Luviri Press is represented outside Africa by:
African Books Collective Oxford (order@africanbookscollective.com)

www.luviripress.blogspot.com

www.africanbookscollective.com

Of Life, Love and Death

Collected Short Stories

Steve Chimombo

Luviri Press

Mzuzu
2021

Dedication

To my short story writing students down the years. I learned more about the craft in those sessions than I could have learned anywhere else.

By the Same Author

Poetry

Napolo and Other Poems (WASI)
Napolo Poems (Manchichi)
Napolo and the Python (Heinemann)
Epic of the Forest Creatures (WASI)
Breaking the Beadstrings (WASI)
Python! Python! (WASI)
The Vipya Poem (WASI)
Ndakatulo za Napolo (Manchichi)

Plays

The Rainmaker (Popular Publications)
Wachiona Ndani? (Dzuka)
Sister! Sister! (WASI)
Achiweni Wani? [translation of *Wachiona Ndani?*] (Manchichi)

Novels

The Basket Girl (Popular Publications)
The Wrath of Napolo (WASI)

Folktales

Caves of Nazimbuli (Popular Publications and Luviri))
Child of Clay (Popular Publications)
Operation Kalulu (Popular Publications and Luviri))
The Bird Boy's Song (WASI and Luviri)

Short Stories

Tell me a Story (Dzuka)
The Hyena Wears Darkness (WASI and Luviri)

Folklore

Malawian Oral Literature (Center for Social Research and Luviri)
Napolo ku Zomba (Manchichi)

Criticism

The Culture of Democracy [with Moira Chimombo] (WASI)
AIDS Artists and Authors (WASI)

General

Directory of Malawian Writing (Dept of Arts and Crafts)

Acknowledgements

Some of the stories collected here have appeared in local and international publications, as follows. "The Rubbish Dump" has been widely anthologized locally and internationally. Among the anthologies are *Contemporary African Short Stories* (Heinemann), *Patterns* (Cappelen) and *Namaluzi* (Dzuka). "~~Taken~~" (reprinted here as "Another Writer ~~Taken~~) appeared in *WASI* and *Under African Eyes* (Farrar Straus and Giroux, Inc.). "A Party for the Dead" appeared in *WASI* and later in *The Unsung Song* (Chancellor College Publications). "Go Back to Your Room" also appeared first in *WASI*, before being included in *Looking for a Rain God and Other Stories from Africa* (Macmillan).

WASI first published the following stories: "MGP505: 10/6/64-25/6/71," "Snakes Eat Mice Too," and "The Blue Room." "Mangadzi Was Here" appeared in *Quest*, and "A Visit to Chikanga" in *The Weekend Nation*.

"The Basket Girl's Mother" was originally written as a short story, but eventually appeared as a chapter in *The Basket Girl* (Popular Publications), a novelette. Similarly, "Burial at Your Own Risk" was integrated into *The Wrath of Napolo* (WASI), a full-fledged novel.

"The Widow's Revenge" and "The Hyena Wears Darkness" were originally written as separate short stories in *WASI*. They found themselves later in *The Hyena Wears Darkness* (WASI), a novelette. The stories were later translated and published in French by Kagni Alem as *L'Ombre de la Hyène* (Ndze).

Table of Contents

Original Introduction

Some of the stories in this collection were molded, if not mutilated, by the oppressive political climate Malawi experienced in the thirty years of Banda's first republic between 1964 and 1994. Some of them could not have been conceived and written during that period without reprisals from the all-powerful Censorship Board, which dictated what could or could not be published. Others were written, but denied publication until the more democratic era after 1994. The shape some of these stories took, then, is not only due to aesthetic considerations but also to non-literary impositions, as the remarks below suggest.

"Another Writer ~~Taken~~" is about a writer detained without trial and the persona's involvement in the event. The story is based on fact and, although the names and places have changed, the original participants have consented to its publication in its present form. The story was suppressed for local and even international publication for obvious reasons. For example, a London editor who knew the prevailing conditions and the main character, regretfully did not dare publish it for fear of what would befall the author. "You must be courageous," he wrote in his rejection slip, "to want to publish this story." I was not being brave, I was frustrated. I knew I had a good story that would not see the light of publication unless the political climate changed.

The oppressive Banda days not only affected the time and place of publication. They affected the form and content of the stories, too. The fact that Malawian poets adopted cryptic and metaphoric strategies to express themselves has been well-documented elsewhere, by both the writers and their critics. What has not been examined is how even the themes were affected. The worst effect is self-censorship, especially on political themes. "MGP505: 10/6/64-25/6/71" is a case in point. Written in the days of harassment by Youth Leaguers, arbitrary arrests by the Special Branch, detention without trial of even innocuous non-political figures, I had several options. Thus it became the story of a lover

8

hounding his rival to prison and forcing him into suicide, the way I had originally heard it from a friend. There was no mention of rival lovers who were party chairmen or cabinet ministers who could fit the role and actually make the story more interesting. Instead, the characters were a harmless returning mine boy and a taxi driver who cooks up the reason for him to be thrown into jail. I didn't change it after the first régime. "Snakes Eat Mice, Too" took on a symbolic mode. Instead of the artist pitting his pen or wits against the oppressive forces, it was a solitary mice-eater who is thwarted in his pursuits by a snake after the same quarry: the mole. These were still interesting writing experiments, but could have been more widely explored. Or the themes could have had deeper implications.

Most people think that the mid-1970s were the peak of Malawi's oppressive years. However, one could feel the impending doom earlier than this. I left the country in 1970 and returned in 1972. My re-entry was quite traumatic. I could not discuss the political situation openly with anyone. Not that I could even do so before I left. Incidents were reported from the mid-1960s of what happened to "dissidents," "subversive elements," or "rebels." Some were forced into exile, others into inarticulacy.

Some of the stories written in the same period had to be on *safe* or *neutral* subjects. They were openly discussed at the Writers Workshop, Chancellor College, although, even then, writing was an unhealthy occupation. The talent seemed to prove one's potential for subversion. In any case, "The Rubbish Dump," the story of a little boy and the garbage collector at the airport was written then. It was non-political and won the first prize in a national short story writing competition. "Another Day at the Office" was also safe, because it concerned the personal suffering of a clerk at home and the work place. Superficially, it had nothing to do with the political realities in the larger world. It was like this to write at the time.

The other stories are recent ones, written toward the end of the period: "A Party for the Dead" commemorates those who die by non-political means, i.e. by road accidents and natural causes, as opposed to those who were *accidentalized* (as some term politically instigated accidents). But then my story is not on that, either. As an aside, a prospective publisher looked at the first collection and rejected it. He said too many stories were on death. I admit, death has received more than its share of space in my short stories. More than half of them are on the theme. How could it be otherwise? We are surrounded by it. Now that AIDS is here to stay, we are reliably told someone is dying every minute globally. How can an author pretend death is not there by eliminating it from or ignoring it in his stories?

You may look at "the widow" series as an extreme example. Once I started on the theme I couldn't stop till three of them were written in the space of two months. I had to stop myself in the third one by attempting a narrative technique I had never attempted in the short story form before. This was to use the dual point of view, thereby stopping each part from forming its own story. By that time, the theme would have been emptied of interest. Forming a trilogy was a firm closure, although there was room for a fourth story, which I keep brushing away firmly.

The collection has been affected by other forms of diminution. The disadvantage of writing in different genres has affected the number of stories that could have gone into this volume. One story is a chapter of my novelette *The Basket Girl* (Popular Publications). Another story appears in *The Wrath of Napolo* (WASI), a novel. Some of my best stories have disappeared from the corpus in this manner. These metamorphoses mean the collection could have demonstrated a richer harvest than the thirty or so years it spans.

On the other hand, the volume has been enriched by a reverse process. Writing in different genres has meant that units that could not be plays, non-fiction, or poetry have been transformed into full-fledged short stories in their own right. The best example is "Mangadzi Was Here." The idea came to me while I was writing *The Rainmaker* (Popular Publications), my first play. It could not be fitted anywhere into the play, and since it came to me as a story, I paused in my playwriting to get it out of my system. I am glad I did.

Yet with all the outward curtailments, I had the freedom to experiment with the form. It was one thing to have an idea, another to clothe it in different garb to make it interesting, yet another to twist it to conform to how one wants to say it. So you will find here the straightforward rendition presented in a slightly nonconformist mode. For example, how could "MGP505" have been presented in a straightforward manner? Or "A Visit to Chikanga" and "The Basket Girl's Mother," with a normal third person point of view? Or the double point of view in "The Hyena Wears Darkness"? I had problems with another prospective editor over the tenses in "A Party for the Dead." He said the story needed editing. The experimentation had backfired on him. I knew what I was doing and why.

So, indeed, short story writing is a fabulous career.

Additional Comments for the Reprint Edition

This reprint is coming at the time of a completely different pandemic, COVID-19, which the late Steve Chimombo has been fortunate to miss. Yet the stories remain entirely relevant, especially those about death related to HIV&AIDS. Just as the characters suffering from HIV&AIDS were stigmatized, so now again we are witnessing the stigmatization of people suffering from COVID-19. Just as during the height of the AIDS pandemic, before the advent of anti-retroviral therapies (ARVs), fake news and fake treatments or even cures proliferated, so now we are seeing a repeat of the same issues. Some of these issues were not mentioned in the original introduction, even though addressed in certain stories, such as gender-based violence and child abuse, but they are proliferating during the current pandemic too.

Truly, good literature remains timeless in its relevance.

Moira Chimombo, July 2021

The Blue Room

1

The first thing Mlenga did when they got home, on Kabula Hill, was to lift 'Mgwetsa,' the new painting, in both hands, like a shield. He turned to face each of the four walls of the lounge, as if in defense.

"We can't hang that in this room." Salima joined him, looking around.

"Why not?" Mlenga flared. "There's enough space for it there, there, and here."

"It's neither the size nor the space." Head tilted to one side, Salima's slender fingers floated over the painting's surface. "See the colours? The shrubbery is brilliantly green in the foreground. The human figures are black. The background has lighter shades of yellow and pink. Blue is the predominant color of the paintings in this room. As you can see, it won't go here."

"All right, it isn't such a great painting anyway, to be in any lounge." Mlenga scrutinized it as if for the first time. "I only bought it for the subject: it's the *mgwetsa*, the rain-calling dance: Makewana, the rain-priestess, in the sacred pool, and Kamundi, the high priest, swimming around her like a python. And there're the Matsano, on the banks clapping hands, with Tsang'oma beating *mbiriwiri*, the sacred drum, on the side. You won't find the religion of our ancestors captured on one canvass like this anywhere else."

"We have the rain queen in the bedroom already."

"I know, but she's all alone in the pool. There's no sense of communal ritual."

"It's much better executed, anyway. Not too realistic and not too abstract to obscure the subject. But it's predominantly brown, even the waters are brown, just imagine. That's why we put it in the bedroom, with the other pieces blending."

Mlenga sighed, he already knew that. In spite of their art-buying sprees being held in consultation with each other, when they got home Salima personally supervised where to hang the paintings, place the sculptures, and locate the carvings. All the pieces aligned themselves to her color or intuitive, sometimes unfathomable, scheme. She pointed, he hung, placed, or located.

"I'll hang this in the study then." That was the only place where he had some control over the décor. It was characterized by its assortedness.

"It'll certainly go well with the prints and the batiks you have there." She went to unpack her weekend things in the bedroom, leaving him standing there like a lone warrior bereft of a target.

They had seen 'Mgwetsa' when they wandered together into the craft shop on their first day at the lakeshore resort where they had gone for the weekend. They had commented on the unusual subject matter, too, but neither had expressed any inclination to purchase it. Nevertheless, as the couple dined and wined, swam and sunbathed away their brief sojourn, Mlenga had toyed with the idea of buying the piece for his wife as a birthday present. When the idea turned into a resolution, he had stolen away to the craft shop just before they checked out. The snag was Salima had caught him paying for it, before the man at the counter had wrapped it up. Salima had also seen him take the package out to their car. She had expressed slight surprise, with Mlenga mumbling something about liking it.

He couldn't reveal to her the real reason he had bought it clandestinely. Not after the reception it had just endured. Mlenga was left now to agonize over what to get her for the day that was only a few weeks away. Salima had institutionalized gift-giving also.

As Salima busied herself in the kitchen afterward, Mlenga, 'Mgwetsa' in hand, went down the hallway. He glanced at the other paintings on both sides. They were punctuated by their children's blown-up photographs. There was Nyangu, the first born, at her graduation. She was now married. There was Damalekani, the second born, about to marry, too. Sizinthera, the last born, was still in college.

Mlenga went into the children's room. It wasn't entirely empty, though: Sizinthera still came home for his mid-terms and vacations. His things were flung around the room: shoes, books, footballs. For want of more space, the parents hung some of their paintings here, too. Their pieces competed with international soccer stars and a wildlife poster, like the ones they had in the toilet.

Mlenga paused below the wildlife poster. A dozen animals: a lion, an elephant, a hippo, a zebra with its young, a buffalo, and so on, stood around in the space allocated to them. There was very little vegetation around them, though.

Mlenga had seen this poster several times before, but had not remarked on its placement among the other artworks. Yet it, too, looked out of place. Salima did not encroach on her son's preserve. She only reigned in the other rooms. Suddenly, something congealed in Mlenga's mind. He left the room precipitately and went into his study.

In some excitement, he leaned 'Mgwetsa' against the wall on top of a book shelf, pulled a chair out and sat down at his desk. He pulled out a blank sheet of paper and started making a rough sketch. He was absorbed in the drawing, until Salima called him for supper. Before joining her, he made a phone call.

"You're Nditha Nzozodo, the wild life painter?" When confirmation came he continued, "I'm Dr Limbani Mlenga. I teach in the university. I have a project for you. Where can we meet to discuss it?"

2

Safari Art Galley was at the end of King George Street, in downtown Blantyre. It gave the impression of being on the high street, yet at the same time set slightly apart from the busiest spots: banks, insurance companies, pharmacies, supermarkets, bookshops, restaurants. It had its own open café, stretching from the *khonde* to spill over into the enclosed garden below it. The customers were usually white expatriates: out-of-town estate owners, contractors, consultants, tourists. Bob Henderson, the proprietor, conducted brisk business in local arts and crafts. No wonder Nzozodo suggested it as their meeting place. He said he was working on something for Henderson.

While waiting for Nzozodo, Mlenga went into the gallery. He found some elderly ladies inside. Most of the pieces were arranged by the artist's name. Nzozodo had a village scene in watercolors. There were some miniature birds in the same medium. Mlenga noted also that Nzozodo preferred the realistic style, with the subjects depicted at ease, as if waiting for the artist to draw them like that. Mlenga wasn't worried about the style. What he had in mind was waiting to evolve with the artist's input.

Apart from the uniformed waiters and the gallery assistants, Mlenga was the only black. So when a tall gangly Malawian walked in, he guessed it was Nzozodo. He wore a checked shirt and faded grey trousers. He looked fifty, but then he could be almost any age after forty, like Mlenga himself.

"Let's sit at the café," Mlenga suggested, after they had introduced themselves to each other. "We can have something to drink and eat as we talk."

"What do you teach at the university?" Nzozodo asked, as they negotiated their way past the other customers, furniture, and potted plants.

"African Literature, but I'm also a writer of sorts. What I teach sometimes impinges upon what I write. This is where you come in. I can paint stories or poems in words, but not on canvass."

Mlenga chose a corner table and motioned to Nzozodo to sit down. A waiter zeroed in on them and took their orders.

"You have probably participated in story-telling when young," Mlenga began.

"Yes," Nzozodo looked perplexed. "At home and in primary school."

"Good. Are you familiar with stories like …?" Mlenga mentioned the common ones. Nzozodo affirmed some. He was not familiar with the creation myths.

"This is what I'd like you to do," Mlenga spread out his sketch on the table. "This is a fireside story-telling scene or supposed to be. I want all the animals and birds in the popular stories in one painting, as I've tried to do here. Each tongue of flame must have at least one story in it. For example, the tug-of-war between the elephant and the hippo, instigated by the hare, is here; pity killed the francolin is here; and so on, till the last flame. Above all the animal characters is the head of the grandmother, who is telling the stories to her grandchildren around her."

"I've never seen anything like this before." Nzozodo wore an awed expression.

"Of course not. Other artists illustrate books or magazines as single-page affairs. The closest they get to this are family trees or village scenes, but those don't tell stories. They're just one-off shots. This is a composite of the major folk stories. Can you do it?"

"I don't know. You see, what I've done before, as you said, is to draw single animals or birds. Even when I bring them together on a poster, I've always conceived of them as separate entities."

Mlenga conceded the point: the posters they had at home did not have any interaction between the animals, even among the same kind. No fighting or gamboling. No hunters or hunted. So how was he going to turn a poster creator into a conflict illustrator? He sat forward.

"Here's your chance to get them interacting, then, as one epic folk story living on your canvass for the first time."

"I'll try."

"Splendid. Anything else we need to discuss before I see your sketches?"

"I'll have to get the materials."

"How much do you need to make a start?"

"We get the canvass from South Africa, through Mr Henderson. But he only does that if there's a big order."

"That'll take too long." Mlenga suddenly looked boyish. "The painting is for my wife. Her birthday is only a few weeks away."

"There's a kind of cotton that does the same work as real canvass. Not many notice the difference, especially with the paint on."

"Then let's support home industry." Mlenga left the sketch and gave him the quoted amount. They arranged to meet again the following week. Mlenga wanted to monitor the first drafts before the artist went full color. He didn't want Salima punching holes in her own present again. He might have lost on 'Mgwetsa,' he didn't want to lose on his own brain-child, this time.

3

In the next few days Mlenga went about his work wondering why he hadn't contacted Nzozodo earlier. It wasn't only through the posters that he knew about the artist. He had attended some of the national exhibitions where Nzozodo's animals and birds also featured. Perhaps it was because he worked in miniatures that Mlenga had kind of passed him over, concentrating on the artists working with larger subjects. Yet Nzozodo was ideal for his project: working in tongues of flames required someone who thought on a small scale.

Working with flames … Mlenga mulled that one over. In the end his heart churned. Flames were orange, weren't they? Or brownish-red? At least reddish-something? So, if he gave Salima the painting she wouldn't hang it in the blue room, after all. His stupendous inspiration would be relegated to another room, maybe the children's.

Mlenga approached the subject of colors circuitously one evening after supper. He made a show of looking at the walls, pausing at each major painting.

"It's not true that this is entirely the blue room," he started warily, like someone in thin clothes venturing out on a chilly day. "Look at the carved map of Africa, there: brown wood. All those village scenes are brown, through and through, like the wood underneath."

"It's away from the angle of vision when you're in the center of the room," she parried.

"What about the chief's stool? All those lions, jackals, and deer clambering in the branches are the color of the base tree: brown."

"It's sitting in its own space, on the floor," she said easily. "It's part of the furniture."

"Exactly." He was targeting the weak points in her defenses. Then he waved his arms dramatically wide: "All this furniture is brown."

"Look at the cushions and the carpet, they're in blue or blends of blue."

Mlenga sighed. Several times a day he'd been seeing what she pointed out since they bought the house and re-designed it to suit their temperaments. More like Salima's, though, he reflected. It had been like this since they had decided to live in wedlock, these titanic tugs of will. One time he'd gain a meter, the next round she'd regain lost ground. Look at the perennial gift-giving competitions she'd seduced him into, again since their love pact. It was now who'd give the other the more endearing and meaningful present. Mlenga decided to retreat to his study.

He hadn't hung 'Mgwetsa' yet. It was still propped on top of the shelf where he had abandoned it a few days before. He glanced at it again: the rain queen and her python priest dominated the scene. They represented the ancient Maravi kingdom's power base. They also represented the male/female balance of power: one came from the Phiri clan, the other from the Bandas. Always. Between them, they ruled the country till the Arab slave traders came. And the British colonizers after them. However, by the time independence from colonial rule was attained, only the ritual powers remained. Those who knew the country's indigenous religion appreciated its meaning without worrying too much about the aesthetics of the piece. He hoped his painting would hold as much import.

He looked at the other pieces in the study. They were quite miscellaneous: a print depicting a popular female dancer, a batik of matchstick women balancing water pots on their heads, a covered fruit bowl, a *bawo* board, a small earthen pot, all bought as the whim caught him, and condemned thereafter to his warren by his wife.

4

Mlenga met Nzozodo again on the *khonde* of Safari Art Gallery. He had a flat rectangular object wrapped in brown paper leaning against the table. He hadn't ordered anything, he had just sat down and waited. Mlenga quickly passed the intervening space, populated by animated groups of whites.

He greeted Nzozodo cheerfully as he joined him. The latter looked a bit distracted as he unwrapped the canvass stretched on a slender frame. He lifted it and wedged it between the table top and their laps so they could view it together, away from curious eyes. Mlenga made some guttural noises as his eyes ranged over the display. His heart contracted as he roved over each flame. The effect of drawing animals and birds in isolation or without connective tissue was evident in each tongue.

"Nzozodo," Mlenga took a deep breath and let it out slowly. "I know you're good at these animals and birds. In fact, they're fantastic. But they're all standing as if they were alone in their individual flames and the other animals around them in the same stories didn't exist."

"I know," the other murmured dispiritedly. "One day someone says: paint me this bird on a tree, I do it. Another day there's a commission for an animal against a certain background, I do it. This time I'm drawing them all on one canvass."

"I was afraid something like this would happen." Mlenga tried to be kind but couldn't hide his disappointment. He pointed out some of the obvious aspects Salima would highlight. "You can see how, at entry point to the left, the hyena faces the viewer instead of the flames. At exit point to the right, the python also faces away from the whole action. Above the flames, the grandmother, who is the controlling figure as the narrator of the stories, gazes vacantly into space. Even the grandchildren are at the same level as the narrator, instead of being around the fire and looking at the source of the stories."

"Fortunately, these faults are easily corrected." Nzozodo was busy making notes. Sometimes he made the alterations right on the canvass as Mlenga talked. Or merely marked where they should occur. "It definitely helps when you point out these things. I'm beginning to see the sketch as it should be, together."

Mlenga fervently hoped so, otherwise Salima would devise devious ways of demonstrating her dissatisfaction every day of their married lives. He decided to approach the problem from a different angle.

"All these stories have something to do with relationships." He felt as if he was once again in the lecture room, propounding a complex literary theory. "For example, the suitor story here has the hyena, who entrusted the hare to be his go-between, instead being turned into a horse and being ridden by the trickster to his beloved, thereby losing the maiden to a friend-now-turned-rival. I don't need to explain this one of pity-killed-the-francolin, every school kid knows it. And so on. There's an underlying unity to the whole thing as I've put it here. It follows the choral chant at fireside stories: '*Tili Tonse*! We're together!' In fact, this is what we're going to call the painting: 'Tili Tonse.' What do you think?"

"It fits perfectly," Nzozodo's eyes flickered, "the way you explain it and the way it looks here, now."

"Wrap 'Tili Tonse' up," Mlenga sighed. "We don't want profane brushes copying it before it's even finished."

Nzozodo got busy. Mlenga gave him a lift to the nearest point to his studio in Njala township. After dropping him, Mlenga drove around aimlessly, his mind seething. He was flagellating himself for not being as good with a brush as he was with a pen. Here he was depending on someone else to translate what was in his mind onto a blank flat surface. Here he was baring the love for his wife to a total stranger to communicate on his behalf through the brush strokes.

By the time Mlenga reached the slopes of Kabula Hill, he had calmed down. He drove up the avenue with high brick walls. The red signs on the metal gates declared: BEWARE OF THE DOG with a motif of a vicious canine or the security company beside it. Mankind withdrawing into fortresses of mansions, lodges, cottages, or palaces. Afraid of relationships? Or nurturing them?

Mlenga blew the car horn in front of his own gates. As he waited for the watchman to open for him, he glanced across to the opposite hill. It was Nyambadwe. It, too, was a low density area, built in the colonial era for the founding British administrators, farmers, missionaries and traders. After independence the educated and rich Malawians simply moved in and continued their lives and histories from these glorified promontories. There were similar places all over Blantyre: Namiwawa, Mount Pleasant, Sunnyside, and so on.

The grating of bolts as the gates opened brought Mlenga back to his surroundings. He nodded to the watchman as he drove past. Sandikonda, their Alsatian, tail wagging, followed his progress along the well-watered garden, luxuriating with different flowers. He drove into the garage. He was home.

5

"We haven't looked at that album for some time," Salima joined Mlenga on the settee one evening. She snuggled against him and put one arm over his shoulder. She inclined her head to have a closer look at the album on his lap.

"We've grown busier as we grew older," he reciprocated the head and shoulder advances, hiding the place he'd been gazing at intently. He flipped the pages to the last entry.

"His features were still congealing." They were looking at Sizinthera, the last-born. "Now he looks just like you."

"Did Nyangu look like you at that age?"

"She was inclined towards her daddy, too. Now she's irretrievably daddy's girl."

"Who did you take after in your teens? I can't remember you showing me your early photos in our college days."

"They tell me I was more like mummy."

"Well, look at what she did to you." He butted her sideways, playfully. "Not like a grandmother-to-be, either."

"The modern girl believes in keeping her figure." She uncoiled herself. "And her beauty sleep. Are you coming?"

"I've got to sort out a few things first." He watched her undulate down the corridor. He waited until he heard the brushing of teeth before resuming scanning the photos.

He hadn't revealed the real reason he had unearthed the albums. He had been cooking up the idea of selecting the best portraits of the family for Nzozodo to put as the human figures in 'Tili Tonse.' Wouldn't it be stunning to have Salima on top with the rest of her brood around her? He wanted the serene, almost mystical expression Salima sometimes wore when relaxed. As for the children, Nzozodo had put two sleek middle-class ones looking as if they were emerging from a white expatriate school. Mlenga had shuddered as he pointed out to the artist that they didn't fit the village fireside setting he knew and wanted faithfully reproduced. Come to think of it, Salima, again, would be too exquisite for the same scene.

It's a hypocritical painting, she'd point out, if he executed his private plans. Not only for the human figures but also on the grounds of veracity. The only time she'd told stories to the kids was in their beds, reading to them in the lounge or in the car, in transit to somewhere. Their fireplace had never seen burning wood, for that matter, only an electric one. We don't want to be living with a fake, she'd aver, thereby rejecting again his carefully conceived creation.

In any case, it wasn't fair to include the family in 'Tili Tonse.' It'd be bribery, as if he was seducing his wife to accept the present for vain

21

reasons. He wanted her to accept it on its own merits. In fact, he looked forward to her initial reactions on first viewing. That is, even before he revealed who it was for and why. Whether or not it hung in the blue room would not matter afterwards.

The blue room! Mlenga was still on the settee, the closed album by his side. He looked at the art collection they had in the lounge again. He could see 'Tili Tonse' on the opposite wall there, among their local masterpieces, lit by its own vibrant colors.

6

By arrangement, Mlenga picked up Nzozodo at a disused filling station near Njala market. Following directions, he turned into a dirt road leading up the slopes into the heart of the township. He was immediately plunged into heaving humanity trampling almost psychedelically in its variegated and colorful second-hand clothes, up and down both sides of the narrow road. Past cabbage, potato, cassava, and tomato sellers; past charcoal, wood, sugarcane, and dried fish sellers. Most of the pedestrians didn't care a car was passing within a few centimeters of their bare feet as the vehicle negotiated potholes and gullies.

Beyond the human hedge were the groceries, bottle stores, and houses built out of unburned bricks. The grey and blackened walls, plastered over with *dambo* sand, peeled and crumbled where they stood, like leprous old men dying on their feet. The roofs made out of rusty iron sheets, some with plastic sacking, were held in place by broken bricks or rocks. Others had tufts of grass growing out of the rubble.

Loud music drilled its notes into Mlenga's eardrums, till his head vibrated like an overfilled bladder aching for release. He went on twisting and straightening, braking and accelerating. He was quite relieved when Nzozodo broke into his ordeal and instructed him to take a side road just as eroded and crowded as the one they were on.

"Park after that grocery. My place is just two houses up."

Mlenga complied. Nzozodo led the way and stopped in front of a metal gate with NKHALANGO ART STUDIO painted on it. An unplastered wall disappeared round the corners on both sides.

"This is my place," Nzozodo said unnecessarily as he opened the gate and entered, his guest following closely. Mlenga found himself in a miniature compound with three semi-detached houses arranged like a T.

"You aren't doing too badly,' Mlenga remarked surveying the place.

The artist gave a shy smile and led him to the left arm of the T, which had another NKHALANGO ART STUDIO on the wall. Mlenga thought *nkhalango*, jungle, was apt for Nzozodo's favorite subjects. They climbed two shallow steps and went in through the open door. The host gestured for Mlenga to sit down, which he did as he cast his eyes round. Paintings—not posters—hung on the walls. Some looked like Nzozodo's watercolors. Others were in acrylic. Wildlife and village scenes predominated. Framed and unframed pieces leaned against each other on the floor.

"I really shouldn't just sit around," Mlenga caught himself. "Let's see how you've got so far."

'Tili Tonse' was propped up on its own stand on one side of the room. They went over to it. Mlenga looked at it critically.

"It's actually a tremendous improvement," was Mlenga's verdict. "The elements are more unified all round."

"I'm glad to hear that," again the shy smile. "My head almost split over it."

"You've done a splendid job."

"Will you want to have a look at it when I'm working with the colors?"

"No, no. From now on, you're on your own. Full colors ahead."

Nzozodo wanted to discuss the kinds of colors he had in mind but Mlenga stopped him again.

"You're the artist," he said firmly. "You know which colors will be suitable for the subject."

Nzozodo walked him back to the car. On parting, Mlenga reminded the artist of the time constraints, but told him to contact him again only if he was satisfied with what he had done. Or if he came up against an unforeseeable problem.

7

Mlenga himself foresaw some of the problems. It was all very well to pronounce that all the elements were now more unified. However, unity went with harmony. Beyond harmony was the artist's personal stamp. Mlenga, yes, Salima, too, would like to see Nzozodo's personal style, not just aesthetics. He hoped that, in full color, Nzozodo would put his elusive individual stamp on 'Tili Tonse'.

He regretted also having given Nzozodo the liberty to use any color. The artist was not privy to his secret ambition to have the painting gain acceptance in the blue room. So how much blue will it contain? Now he had missed the opportunity to suggest liberal splashes of blue and its blends.

The days went by with Mlenga tormenting himself like this. He stopped himself from actually visiting the artist on some pretext or other. When Nzozodo phoned at last for him to collect the painting, he abandoned everything he was doing.

He found Nzozodo in his studio with 'Tili Tonse' on display. He caught his breath. It was amazing what a brush of color could do to a pencil sketch.

"What do you think of it yourself?"

"It's a bullet!" Nzozodo replied ambiguously. "Once I started seeing everything together in my mind, I just went like that."

Mlenga refrained from looking at it with Salima's eyes. Whether or not she accepted it didn't alter the fact that he liked it. Even the grandmother had a blue headdress, making her stand out from the lighter shade of the skies around her.

"This is fantastic." Mlenga breathed finally. "How long will it take for you to frame it?"

"With the borders, two hours."

"I'll be back in that time."

Nzozodo had already wrapped it up by the time he returned. They strapped it in the back of the car. When they finished Mlenga felt like hugging the artist.

"What we artists need are the themes." Nzozodo issued his shy smile again. "You gave me solid themes and I worked on them."

"There's more from where those came," were Mlenga's parting words. "You'll be seeing more of me now."

Mlenga drove slowly back home. He unloaded 'Tili Tonse' and paused just inside the front door. Salima was still out. Great. He wanted a temporary display place for it to be the first thing she saw when she entered through the front door.

When Mlenga heard her drive in, he positioned himself away from the painting not to distract her. The car door shut. Footsteps on the *khonde*. Door opening.

"What's this?" She stopped short.

"The latest acquisition."

Small furrows on her forehead, her eyes ran over it.

"The flames are too defined, they should fade into each other."

Mlenga had felt so too, in a vague sort of way but had not articulated it to the artist.

"The details of the animals and birds are brilliant. But they're too distinct. They're like our musicians, loud at the same time, drowning each other out, wanting to draw attention to themselves. They should be as if coming out of the grandmother's mind."

Mlenga's heart was cascading.

"Where shall we hang this?"

"I don't know." His heart speared his insides. "You …"

"We'll have to shift the map of Africa so it's next to the window."

"I had thought so, too." Mlenga couldn't wait to execute the orders. "It's meant to be your birthday gift."

"After all the nasty things I said about it?" She craned her neck. "The kids look cute. Do you think I'll reach the age of the grandmother to tell stories to our own?"

She drew closer to him and melted in his arms.

Mangadzi Was Here

Kamundi drove slowly over the bridge traversing the river Mzimundilinde. When he had first heard the name, he had enquired from a friend why it was so called. The story behind Mzimundilinde, spirit-wait-for-me, was a bit far-fetched, he thought.

About thirty years ago, the man said, there was no bridge where Kamundi was now driving. Instead there were only large rocks which were used if one wanted to get to the other side. There wouldn't have been any need to ask why the river was called Mzimundilinde then, for only a hundred yards below the bridge was a large deep pool which had been inhabited by water spirits. On a quiet afternoon you could see some of their manifestations. Sometimes even hands mysteriously emerged from the dark depths as though about to receive some invisible gift from the sky.

Why weren't there any spirits now, as of old, Kamundi had enquired, with a faint smile of skepticism. The man had said the white man with his cars, roads and bridges had driven them away. The spirits had fled to the mountain of Mtalika, the source of the river. But before the white man had turned everything upside down, Napolo had warned them of the disturbance.

And who, or what, was Napolo, Kamundi had enquired, exasperated. Napolo, he was told in a surprised tone, why, Napolo was the huge snake that lived under Mtalika mountain; that time, Napolo traveled underground to drink from the lake. He passed here and forewarned the spirits of what was to come. Napolo was still at the lake, but would return to his abode in the mountains soon. Could Kamundi not see for himself that Mtalika was tilted on one side? The part that had subsided would right itself when Napolo returned to live under it.

Kamundi changed into second gear as he climbed the small hill after the bridge. He shrugged his shoulders again, as he had done when the old man had told him about Mzimundilinde. Kamundi had never ceased to be amazed to what lengths the simple, superstitious mind will go to explain natural phenomena. The play of light on water can produce remarkable effects which could look like human forms. Anyone could tell that, without getting nameless terrors at the sight. And Napolo, however cataclysmic, what was Napolo but a landslide? There had been numerous landslides in the country. The last major one was thirty years ago, as the man had said. But according to the meteorological reports, the abundant rainfall of that year was caused by a deflected cyclone coming from Mozambique to the east of the country. Kamundi had checked on that. A huge snake, indeed!

As Kamundi reached the top of the hill, the cliffs of Mtalika mountain came into view. The greyish blue crags rising on the shoulders of the thick forests under them looked formidable enough. The early inhabitants must have had fun creating myths about the inscrutable mask that looked like a gigantic deity brooding over puny mortals. Any tilt of the mountain was a pure figment of the imagination. Whoever heard of a mountain built according to the principals of mathematics anyhow?

The road Kamundi took ran parallel to the cliffs and the sun would plunge behind them within an hour or so. Living on the slopes of a mountain as high as nine thousand feet only meant darkness descended prematurely and with a devastating suddenness that paralyzed those not used to it. There wasn't even the ghost of the celebrated brevity of a tropical twilight. Here, at least, there was an almost palpable division between day and night.

He drove through the main residential area of the town's upper class and aspiring well-to-do. Well clipped hedges hid neat little gardens growing geraniums, frangipane, or roses. Bougainvillea snaked up poles, to writhe uncertainly on the iron roofs. Telegraph poles punctuated Kamundi's progress through avenues flanked by flamboyant or jacaranda trees. As he passed 2nd Avenue he thought the Ministry of Works was playing a practical joke on the population; especially when he came across a road works sign that announced unabashed: DEVIATION. There was, Kamundi thought, something ironically comic about modernity.

Kamundi took his bearings from the sun over the mountain. The northern edge of the residential area would be directly in front of him. He drove for another two minutes, looking for the last house. This was revealed to be an ugly structure of green roofing and sickly white walls, all angles and no sense. A European life-style had its attractions for some people, which made them live in such houses as these.

The girl had said: after the last house, there was no road. He would find a path leading to the villages.

Kamundi, drawing to a halt, parked his car by the roadside. He switched off the engine, looked into the interior driving mirror and noticed droplets of sweat on his forehead. He took off his jacket and tie, and placed them on the back seat. He had an irresistible impulse to take off all his clothes and go naked along the bushy track. Which would be silly, he thought. Streaking would be ridiculous, even in the village setting. And what would Mangadzi's reaction be, if she saw Kamundi approaching, dangling his what's-it. That was no way of winning friends or influencing people. Certainly not a prospective girlfriend and her parents.

He checked himself as he locked the car. Prospective girlfriend was a new one. He hadn't seriously thought of having Mangadzi as a girlfriend. He was only fulfilling a promise that he would visit her in the village. A rash promise made in the height of bravado? Well, the girl had certainly dared him to visit her in the village. The West had eaten him completely, she had accused him, town-dweller that he was, and the town maggots would be the ones to feed on him in the end. Kamundi had emphatically told her he would be saying "Odi" at her home after work the following day. She had only smiled enigmatically. As he had walked away from her, he thought he heard her mumble something like, "I will be waiting for you," which had struck Kamundi as odd. They had only met that day— for only thirty or so minutes in fact.

And here he was beating the dust to see her again. What terrible fascination was in this village girl that had drawn a thirty-year-old bachelor from the glamorous snare of the town in hot pursuit? Kamundi mused as he walked along the path. He seemed to have left the sounds of the town far behind. Not even the sound of a car penetrated the forest where the wild birds rioted in the branches. He couldn't remember the names of all of them. Some bird cries were familiar from his childhood days in his own village. Was that a *pumbwa* or a *njiwa*? He gave up. The only bird noises he could distinctly recognize were the crows in the town's market place.

When you have crossed the ravine, the girl had told him, you'll know you're near the village I come from. Ask for Mangadzi. Everybody knows her there. Kamundi had nodded. Such beauty as hers would stick out a mile.

Kamundi stopped for a moment to gaze at the small pool of water which had collected among the rocks before rippling away downstream in the ravine. Tall *mombo* and *nkuyu* trees made a natural roof overhead with their overhanging branches. It was a cool, restful place to retire to occasionally. If one had the time.

This pool reminded him of the other, larger one at Mzimundilinde, where he had first met Mangadzi. It was Sunday and Kamundi had got bored sitting alone at home listening to the afternoon programs on the radio. He decided to go for a drive. He had no specific place in mind, but found himself near Mzimundilinde. He had parked the car on the main road and walked a short distance to where the man had said the pool was.

There hadn't been anything extraordinary about that pool. It was about ten feet wide and deep enough to be a miniature natural swimming pool. An accumulation of dried bits and pieces of left-over food and fruit commemorated the fact that somebody had thought so already. The water came in a small cataract of about five feet plunging down a huge boulder. The urge to take off his clothes and take a plunge gripped Kamundi. He resisted the temptation, for the main road was only a hundred yards away and anyone who cared to look would see him splashing about. Not that he cared.

He gave up the attempt to see any spirits in the depths of the pool and was turning to go back when he noticed the girl, or rather, the young woman, on one of the rocks near the cataract.

"Hello," Kamundi surprised himself. "Are you looking for spirits too?"

"*Chiani?*" the girl had replied in the vernacular.

Kamundi was vaguely disappointed but switched into the vernacular. "I said," he repeated, "are you looking for the spirits too?"

"*Mizimu?*"

29

The cataract drowned some of the words, so Kamundi decided to climb the rocks that separated them. The girl watched him as he balanced himself on them and placed an elegantly trousered leg on the rock next to her. He noticed that his brown leather shoes had caught the spray as he came up.

She did not move, but kept her pose: one arm across her middle supporting the elbow of the other, with its palm cupping her chin. Bare feet peeped from under the hem of the dress she wore. She looked as fresh as if she had just emerged from a dip in the water below.

"What were you saying?" She looked up at him. Her eyes were as clear and deep as the pool below. She seemed to see into and beyond him, far into the great distance.

"It is said," Kamundi felt himself drowning in those eyes, "this pool was once inhabited by spirits."

"What kind of spirits?"

"I don't know," Kamundi replied. "Water spirits, nature spirits, or whatever it is they are called. I'm not acquainted with them so I wouldn't know how to classify them."

"That is interesting," she remarked.

Kamundi had been trying to place her. As she was seated, it was difficult to tell what kind of dress she was wearing. Her slightly oval face, light brown skin, limpid eyes, and full, rich lips were not enough to go by. She could be from any part of the country. The accent helped more. It could only mean she came from the south. It wasn't one he had met except on one or two occasions when he was talking to people who obviously came from the villages on the outskirts of the town.

"Anyhow," Kamundi went on, "we won't see any these days."

"Why not?"

"It seems the white man's cars, tarmac, and concrete bridges have chased our neighbors away."

"What a pity!"

"Yes, although Napolo, I'm told, had a hand in it. He warned them before, to move house."

"You seem to know quite a lot about this place."

"Not really. Only scraps from my superstitious friends."

"Don't you believe it?"

"Hardly. I was brought up in a very different way and learned to scoff at these things."

The spray from the cataract made a small rainbow in the sun that seemed to start from somewhere above her and end in the water below.

"You've got a rainbow on your head."

"Have I?" She smiled faintly and looked about her.

Kamundi wanted to get her talking. She had a melodious voice that blended harmoniously with the noise of the water plunging below. When she smiled, Kamundi likened her teeth to ripe maize grain, and was amused by the comparison. She certainly was a ripe woman.

She still hadn't moved, except that instant when she had turned her neck to look around her. Kamundi wished he had brought his camera. The picture she made was worth capturing. She looked part of the water, the trees, the breeze ... Kamundi thought she could be the stuff goddesses and pagan religions were made of. A pity about the camera ...

"Yes." Kamundi gazed at her again. "It's a beautiful effect. By the way, what's your name?"

"Mangadzi."

"Mangadzi?" Kamundi worked it over in his mind. "That's an unusual name. Most girls I've met are Mary, Rose, or some such ordinary name."

"I don't find it unusual."

"I'm sorry," Kamundi said quickly, "I didn't mean to be rude."

"What's yours?"

"Kamundi."

"Why?"

They both laughed.

"Tell me," Kamundi ventured, "what are you doing here?"

"I live near here," she waved an arm vaguely, "and sometimes I come and sit on the rocks. I find it restful."

"I thought it was only the leisured class who suffered from that disease."

"Hm?"

"Let it pass. Where do you come from?"

"Near those villages at the edge of those white men's houses."

31

"I live in one of those," Kamundi teased, "but I am definitely not a white man."

"No," Mangadzi's eyes showed an indecipherable emotion, "but white man is in everything about you: shoes, clothes, and you seem to be having difficulty speaking your own language."

"I know." Kamundi loved those flashing eyes. "I've lived too long in the white man's world."

"Townsman," Mangadzi spat out. "Tell me, when were you last in your village?"

"Some time ago." Kamundi wondered why he should have to defend himself against this strange woman. "I confess there isn't much for me to do there."

"Do you think so?"

The question reared its face between them. Kamundi was getting more and more troubled.

"I don't know."

"I suppose you didn't even know that there are villages next to those white men's houses?"

"I've always meant to call on my neighbors there," Kamundi said helplessly. Then, as the idea took a firm root, "Look, can I come and visit you at your home?"

"No."

"Why not?"

"Why?"

"I feel I must."

"Why?"

"Well, I'd like to see you again."

"Why?"

"I don't know."

They went on like that until Kamundi thought it was all lunacy. But in the end, Mangadzi said he could, strangers though they were. Kamundi had told her he felt as though they had known each other a long time.

He had left her there on the rocks. She looked like a picture of an Egyptian goddess he had seen in a history book at the university. He was intrigued by her bearing. She wore an air of profound anguish mingled with patience. Kamundi thought, as he passed below it, the cataract was reminiscent of the beat of many drums. He glanced back at her. The rainbow effect was quite dazzling. *Uta-wa-leza*: God's bow. Strange how light can play such tricks in the world.

Kamundi had spent a very restless night at home. Each time he thought about Mangadzi, he was struck by the improbable meeting and her altogether inexplicable presence on the rocks. Seen in the cold light of the next morning, her image still held that haunting, indefinable, tragic aura. There seemed a certain passionate wildness in her words. And Kamundi could only wonder what strange fate had brought them together.

During breakfast, he noticed with gloom how empty his house was. The furniture stared back at him bleakly and lifelessly against the white of the walls. The morning show on the radio repeated jokes he had heard a thousand times before. The music echoed back from the bare bachelor walls. Kamundi threw the tasteless eggs he had been chewing into the kitchen bucket. He had only a cup of tea and left for his office.

Working in an executive position allowed his mind to wander most of the day. The refrain: I shall be waiting for you, mingled with the roll of drums from the cataract, haunted his day. No girl had ever made such a deep impression on him before. The Marys, Annies, and Roses had shied away as soon as they had detected that air of someone waiting for something to come one day. But not them …

Kamundi knelt on a rock at the edge of the pool and was washing his face in the cool mountain water when he heard the tap of a stick on a rock.

"Zikomo."

"Eee." Kamundi straightened up and saw a very old woman in a *biriwita* going carefully over the rocks.

"Excuse me, mother."

"Yes, my son?" She paused.

"Do you come from the next village?"

"Ye-e-s."

"Oh, good." Kamundi stood up. "Do you know the house of er-er Mangadzi?"

"Mangadzi?" she echoed. "Ye-e-s. Why, do you know her?"

"Er-er." Kamundi was confused. "I am going to see her people. I have never been there before."

"I am going to the village myself." The woman smiled toothlessly. "I could show you where she lives."

"Thank you very much."

"Lead on, then." The woman gestured. "I shall follow behind. These bones of mine can't move as fast as yours."

Kamundi was excited and relieved. At least he wouldn't have to waste time asking numerous people where Mangadzi lived. This was more discreet.

Kamundi thought they were moving too slowly for his liking. But at least the old woman wasn't talkative, for which he was thankful. She tapped her way slowly behind him till they came upon the village. Children ran about playing their mysterious games. Somewhere to their left a song accompanied by a *thwack!* announced a woman pounding grain. Small, round, grass-thatched huts sprawled on both sides of the path. Groups of men and women on the *khondes* sat either talking or working at something. A few paused to watch their passage.

Kamundi was taken back to his childhood at his own village. It gave him a strange sensation of release and relief to hear familiar sounds he thought he had long left behind.

A little boy, half-naked, crossed their path at great speed, stopped abruptly and stuck out a grimy hand.

"*Moni!*"

"*Moni!*" Kamundi cheerfully offered his hand. He was home.

The boy watched them pass with expressionless eyes and sped out of sight again. He too was like that once.

Kamundi glanced back at the old woman. She seemed to have forgotten her mission, for they were now proceeding out of the village. He looked uneasily at the sky. The atmosphere had that ominous stillness of an impending storm. Dark clouds had already formed, obscuring the setting sun. The air, now slightly brown, shimmered intensely. They would be plunged in darkness any minute now—if not rain.

He wished the old woman would hurry or say something. He cursed himself for not having brought a torch. It would have helped him on his solitary trek back through those bewildering little paths they had taken. Or an umbrella.

The unsteady tap, tap of the woman drew closer to him, as he tried again to get his bearings. They had left the village behind now. A few yards to the right he recognized a cluster of *nkhadzi* trees. That would be the village graveyard, he thought, and as if to confirm his suspicions, an owl hooted up in a tree, *whoo! whoo!* Kamundi suddenly felt the hair stirring at the back of his neck. The old woman's voice broke the silence, and it made him tremble violently.

"Wait for me," she quavered. "I'm not as young as the Mangadzi you know."

"I'm sorry, mother." He stopped and waited.

Kamundi was surprised at the faintness of his voice. He suddenly felt he was in the presence of something he could not fathom. The black form of the old woman drew eerily nearer and stopped a few feet from him. The entrance to the graveyard yawned darkly to the right.

The old woman chuckled quietly in the gloom.

"Do you know why she was called Mangadzi?"

"No," Kamundi said curtly. What he wanted to know was where he could find her. But strangely enough he liked the old woman, although she was apt to give one the creeps.

"She," she continued, "is named after Makewana, the mother of all mankind."

"Why?"

"You should know, Kamundi."

"Me?"

"Yes. Don't you know Kamundi was the python-priest of Makewana?"

"Was he?"

"Stop calling me 'mother'!" She drew closer to him. "I'm Mangadzi and you are my python-priest, Kamundi. I've been waiting for you, my husband. Come, let's go back to where we belong. This world doesn't need us anymore ...."

She led the way to the graveyard.

The Basket Girl's Mother

I was sitting at a corner table in the private room of Mtalika View Bar, with a foaming beer and an open newspaper in front of me. I glanced occasionally at the three executive types at the next table, filled with almost a crateful of both empty and full bottles. Their talk grew louder and louder as the Saturday afternoon advanced. I could not help overhearing what they were saying: they were so near. I could have touched one of them if I'd stretched out a hand or a foot.

It started with the one called Jo turning to the third one. "Do you know where the name Shaibu came from, Tom?"

"His great grandfather was a fanatical Moslem."

"Religion has nothing to do with it," Jo shook his head solemnly. "There was this white man who, on a sudden impulse, invited his black servant to a party. There weren't many blacks there, so the poor boy was a fish out of water. When the master noticed this, he grew very concerned, gave him another drink, and asked 'Are you shy, boy?' The boy turned to another black face and announced joyfully, *'Bwana kundenda "shy boy", basi kutandila lelo uneji "Shaibu"'.*"

Jo was the most talkative of the group. It seemed the other two did not mind. The way they acted, Jo appeared to be a great fellow to have around.

"Your grandfather was a medicine man, wasn't he, Shaibu?" Jo persisted. It was just not Shaibu's day.

"Don't forget your mother had to go to him to have you pulled out of her womb," Shaibu retaliated.

"I know," Jo was imperturbable. "We great people start creating problems from an early age."

Shaibu snorted. Tom joined him. Jo ignored them and continued on a more serious note.

"One of these days, I'm going to write the story of Wina the Basket Girl in the conventional manner. All the tricks of the trade—well, almost —will be included: depth of characterization, intricate plot, a realized setting in time and space, a credible point of view, overlap of themes, the appropriate language style, *à la* Jo."

I sat up at the mention of Wina, and listened more attentively. Shaibu put on a solemn air and winked ostentatiously at Tom. He winked back.

"As it is," Jo ignored the winks again, "I have only the raw material, which is as follows. I see the setting as Mtalika View Bar, which is, of course, where it all started. The inmates of the bar—customers, bargirls, barmen, and even the owner—do the usual rounds; drinking themselves to death, catching STIs, fighting over new bargirls. The customers are drawn from different strata of the society: civil servants, businessmen, lecturers, soldiers, the police. They are all involved in the dynamics of this community. All of them are ridden with the fears, worries, and insecurities that a place like this pretends to dispel."

I stopped reading entirely and pricked up my ears, although I pretended not to be listening. Wina, the basket girl, was the only reason I had come to the place. Not to find her, but her mother, who used to work here ages ago. I had tried to find out where she lived, but drew a blank. My only lead was to wait for the day she chose to drop into the Bar. She had stopped working, I was told, being now too old for the game. However, she still haunted it for old time's sake, the proprietor had assured me.

"One hot evening," Jo's even voice floated above the general background noise, "a respectable gentleman just happened to drop in for a quick drink. He'd never been to the place before. He was so well-positioned in society he couldn't be seen dead in a place like this. His presence was as inexplicable as the subsequent events he got involved in."

The proprietor came in and beamed at everyone.

"Ah, my friends." He shook hands with each one. "You are welcome, very, very welcome. It gives my humble place some prestige to have you people dropping in like this. Not many people come at the corner of the month. Most people are broke and stay at home."

"We're just passing through." Jo acted as the spokesman.

"We're on our way to see Shaibu's sick grandmother."

"Nothing serious, I hope," the proprietor was gloomy.

"We hope not."

"Any way," he turned to go, "enjoy yourselves. Feel at home."

"Thanks."

"She hasn't come yet." The proprietor answered my enquiring look as he passed my table to go out.

"I don't like fellows taking liberties with my grandmother," Shaibu complained to Jo.

"I had to get rid of that fellow," Jo explained blandly. "He'd have wanted to join us in no time."

"Why didn't you mention your own grandmother?"

"Because she isn't sick."

"But nor is mine."

"Let Jo continue with the story," Tom intervened.

"As I was saying," Jo should have been on the stage, "the story started in similar circumstances: a respectable husband belonging to the higher echelons of society, and an irresistible prostitute."

"A touch of mystery and romance." Tom nodded his head.

"If you ask me," Shaibu put in, "it's the same old, overworked theme of the dangerous fascination prostitutes have for respectable folk."

"This will have a fresh and original slant," Jo protested.

"If there is one," Shaibu got up, "I don't see it. Look, do you want another beer, because I'd like one. These would-be story-tellers give me a huge thirst."

"I'll have another one," Jo said blandly. "Thank you. I'm just warming up."

"I'll have a break then, if you don't mind."

"Go ahead," Jo waved him away. "The GENTS is to your left after the LADIES."

Shaibu glared at him and stormed out.

"The respectable gentleman," Jo resumed the story.

"What's his name, for God's sake?" Tom enquired.

"The name is not important: his position, respectability, faithfulness, and all the gentility of his class are more important. The kind of gentleman you would meet at openings of parliament, alumni reunions, inaugurations, charity balls, or sponsored walks. You know, the pinstriped suit, chauffeur-driven type who stays at all-expenses-paid hotels while on familiarization tours round the world. He made the society and the society made him."

The door opened again to admit an elderly woman in flashy imported clothes, a glass in hand. Her age made her seem out of place, yet her manner declared that she was at home. She glanced carelessly round the room, not looking for anyone or anything in particular. She came to a decision and sat down opposite me. I wondered if it was Margaret. I had never met her, and could not recognize her from the description the proprietor had given me. I did not want to ask him yet: I wanted to hear the rest of the story from the next table. It seemed a matter of life and death to let Jo finish telling it.

"Obviously," Jo inclined his head, "the story would lose some of its impact if it was told from the basket girl's point of view Technically, too, it would make it incredible, if not impossible: after all she is the product of the accidental meeting of this gentleman and the prostitute."

"I suppose," Tom was toying with his glass, "the prostitute's name is not important, either."

"It is not: the meeting of the two is more crucial."

The woman across the table took a long pull from her glass and started playing with a packet of cigarettes and a box of matches which she had taken out of her handbag. She had not smoked since coming in and sitting down.

"The story can't be told from the prostitute's point of view either. A victim's story, especially a bargirl's is not free from bias or self-interest."

"But if the meeting was purely accidental," Tom pointed out, "who was the real victim?"

"That's just it: both participants are willing victims of circumstance; sympathy here seems to be shared between the exploiter and the exploited."

"How can that be? One is clearly the exploiter, who cannot be sympathized with, however extenuating the circumstances."

"We shall never know the circumstances which brought him to her in the first place. What we do know is that a girl was born, grew up as a basket girl the first ten or so years of her life, before the gentleman adopted her."

I forgot to call for the refill to my glass as the story unfolded. Jo seemed to know as much as I did of Wina's past life. I was wondering how I was going to declare my involvement in it to these total strangers when Shaibu came back.

"He is still at it, is he?" Shaibu laughed, as he reclaimed his seat.

"How did he know it was his own daughter?" Tom was still interested, if Shaibu was not.

"That's another strand whose full details we shall never know. Maybe we don't need those details for the story to be written. What is important is that the true parentage was revealed and the daughter was reunited with her father."

"Who is the father?" It was Shaibu's turn to be exasperated.

"He's dead," I said.

I have never seen necks swivel like directors' chairs, as those three heads turned to look at me, with various degrees of shock, surprise, and disbelief. I, too, was surprised. Since coming into the room, I had not uttered a word to anyone, beyond calling for refills from the several waitresses coming in and out. What prompted me to come out into the open was the feeling that it was now or never. If I lost the opportunity, I might not get further leads to my quest.

"He died exactly ten years ago today." I showed the "IN MEMORIAM" page to them. "There's the proof."

They craned round the small item I had been reading over and over in the room while they talked and drank. They read:

IN MEMORIAM

Days, weeks, months, and years have now turned into a decade today since you closed your eyes for eternal rest. The anguish of your unexpected departure haunts our lives. Our hearts are still filled with sorrow and memories of your brief stay. You left a gap impossible to fill. We loved you, but Chiuta loved you most. You will always be missed by your wife, Taona, and children, Win and Wina.

"How did you know Jo was talking about him?" Shaibu asked me suspiciously.

"As Jo said, it happened in this very place, between respectable and not so respectable members of the society. The product was a basket girl who was later adopted by the father. There is only one person who did that in the last twenty or so years in Mtalika Town. That's him."

"What's your interest in the story?" Jo asked me.

"Very simple." I pulled up my chair between Jo and Shaibu. "I'm a friend of the family. In fact, I came here looking for the girl's mother."

"But this happened more than twenty years ago," Jo frowned in his glass.

"Exactly," I said warmly. "I got a letter from the girl asking me to find her mother. It seems there has been a breakdown in communication, and she needs to know whether or not she's dead before doing anything else."

"Like what?" Tom asked across the table.

"Well," I had not wanted to become the narrator of the basket girl's story, but went on, "She's in the States at the moment and it'd be expensive to come here to find out for herself, wouldn't it?"

"Doesn't she want to visit her own mother?" Shaibu was still suspicious of me. It grated on my nerves.

"She can't come and go just like that, you know. It's a long way for luxury self-paid trips. In any case, the point is that she needs news of her mother urgently."

"Why don't you ask her mother, then?"

"I've been trying to trace her in the past few weeks."

The proprietor breezed in again. "Have you introduced yourselves?" He looked at the woman at my previous table and then at me.

"That ... that's Wina's mother?" I half sat up.

"That is Margaret," the proprietor beamed at me. "The one you were looking for."

"Are you Wina's mother?" I switched to the vernacular, getting up and going round to her chair.

"I am Margaret." She was half tipsy. "Are you the one looking for me?"

41

I nodded as I pulled my chair back to the table and placed it near her. I looked at her more closely. She was the right age to be Wina's mother.

"Buy me a drink."

The proprietor waved a waitress to our table. "Well," he turned to go, "enjoy yourselves."

I ordered two drinks.

"No." I changed my mind. "Give these gentlemen another round, too."

"For he's a jolly good fellow," Shaibu sang loudly off-key.

"So you know my baby?" Margaret's words were slightly slurred.

"I'm Wina's friend."

"I don't know you."

"You wouldn't know me. I was too young for you to know me. Wina and her brother and I went to the same school."

"She ran away from me."

"She had to go to school abroad."

"But she never came back."

"I hear she went to Europe, Britain, and now she's in the States."

"That's why I'm saying she ran away from me. She didn't want to have a prostitute for her mother."

"I'm sure that's not the real reason."

"I know what I'm saying." She paused to take a drink the waitress had placed noisily in front of her.

The other table had now suspended its activities and was listening avidly. The waitress put their drinks in front of them. They raised their glasses to me. I reciprocated.

"As she grew up," Margaret continued with the slight slur, "I could see it in her eyes: she was ashamed of me."

"She was an honest, sensitive, and sensible girl," I protested.

"At first, yes, when she was under my care. As a basket girl, she was sweet, kind, and loving. She'd bring all her daily takings for me to keep for her. She was loving to her father, too. Even before they knew their true relationship, she would pick *thelele la denje* for him almost every week. I bet he grew tired of the stuff. Anyway, he took her away from me and

42

lived with her on the slopes of Mtalika Mountain. Although she used to still come and see me, things started to change."

"What things?" Shaibu asked across the intervening space.

"At first she used to spend the weekends with me, I mean sleep at my place, help me at home, and all that. I had to stop her by saying that her father would take me to court, since I had signed papers promising to lay no claim to her in future."

"But surely," Shaibu said almost truculently, "the father understood the emotional ties that bound you together? Ties that could not be signed away on legal documents?"

"He understood that all right. He was a very understanding man. But you see, he and I knew that Wina was not my daughter."

"What!" The spontaneous reaction was as electrifying as the time I had come into the conversation. It was explosive news to me too.

"Rose," Margaret said, almost tearfully, "my friend, Rose, was the real mother. She died in child-birth."

There were loud sympathetic noises from the next table. We paused, took long swigs, but turned almost desperately back to Margaret for more information.

"That's why I couldn't really claim her at any time, although I'd brought her up myself, single-handed. And loved her dearly—Chauta knows how much I loved her. I gave her away to her father to save her from the streets and the bars. I didn't want her to end up like me or her mother, the spirits rest her soul."

"But still, she used to visit you all the same," I persisted.

"As she grew older and more aware of the nature of my work, my work place, her father and his position, her visits became briefer and less frequent. She didn't even tell me she was leaving the country."

"How did you know then?"

"Her father told me."

"He still kept in touch with you?"

"He was a gentleman." A few tears rolled down her cheeks this time. "He knew what I had been through to bring up Wina and helped me in every way he could."

43

The newspaper write-up at his death came to my mind. I remembered phrases like "a highly-placed citizen," "devoted his time, intellect, and interest to the civic affairs of his country," "a public servant."

"He continued to visit you?" Shaibu thrust in again, viciously.

I saw Jo stamp on Shaibu's foot under the table. Shaibu glared into his glass.

"He was trying to help me, can't you see? He built me a house. He even tried to persuade me to stop working here, but I couldn't. Mtalika View Bar was all the life I knew. I couldn't—still can't resist the place. It's my whole life. It's made me what I am, and it made Wina."

"Wina sent me to find you." I tried to change the direction the story had taken.

"How come she asked for you to find me?"

"As I explained before, I'm a family friend. She grew worried when you stopped answering her letters."

"How could I keep answering her letters when she ran away from me? What could I say to her? That I wanted her back?"

"That would at least tell her you still cared."

"I cared for that kid." She stopped suddenly, reached for her bag, opened it, fumbled in an inside pocket, and took out a small photo.

"There's your girl." She thrust a print at me. "I still keep her pictures, you see."

I anxiously turned it the right way up and gazed at the full-blown Afro-hair head tilted at just the right angle before it became a challenge. The limpid eyes of a girl in her early twenties smiled back at me. Full, well-rounded lips and a pert nose completed a picture of a perfectly formed head. The effect was dazzling, devastating. I could hardly contain the mounting excitement. I had not seen Wina since she left the country. And now here she was, my first love, ripe and ready somewhere in New York. I reluctantly, almost jealously, permitted the others to take a peek at my goddess. I watched the progress of the print impatiently as it passed from hand to hand, imagining the beer stains and grease accumulating on it before it got back.

"Whew!" Shaibu whistled as he held my Wina. "Where is this dream girl?"

If I found Shaibu objectionable before, it was confirmed now. I tried to shake off the feeling: it was only a picture, the real body being thousands of miles away: I would have reacted the same way as Shaibu if I saw such exquisitely modelled features on a total stranger anywhere. I kept reassuring myself.

I snatched the photo back from Shaibu, looked at it tenderly again, before giving it back to Margaret.

"Do you know where she is now?" I asked.

"The last letter was from New York still."

"I know she's still there. I meant the exact address."

"I thought you said she wrote you." Shaibu was at me again. I started nursing a deep hatred for him.

"Yes, but she didn't give me her present address."

"That's strange."

"She's a strange girl." I glowered at Shaibu. I was smarting and I could not explain or hide my embarrassment as I felt an explanation was needed. "She deliberately left out the address so that I could not trace her."

"Why not?" A very unkind question.

I figured I was in danger of losing credibility if I continued with Shaibu. I turned to Margaret and concentrated on her. "She said I could get it from you. She figured if I found you and you gave me her address, then you were alive and well."

"And if not?"

"She would not have anything more to do with this country if you were dead."

"As you said," Jo said after a short silence, "she sure is a strange girl. I thought you said she had a brother?"

"Yes, but he's incommunicado."

"What happened?"

"I don't need to go into that at the moment. It's rather delicate. Anyway, Wina doesn't know the fate of her brother, either. All the more reason to get in touch with her."

"What about her—is it second?—stepmother?" Tom was pursuing a line that had also occurred to me. "She must have been the one who put the 'In memoriam' in the papers."

"She, too, is dead." I shook my head.

"Then who …?"

"Wina."

"The paper will have her address, then."

"No lead there, either. I tried it already. They got the instructions, the item, and a local check in the mail, with Wina's father's old address on it."

"Whew!" Shaibu whistled again. "I'd sure like to meet that girl some day."

"I'm going to see her next month." I glared at him.

"How is that?" A sea of incredulous faces.

"I'm going to the States. That's why it's important for me to get her address."

"What if I don't give it to you, lover boy?" Margaret had sensed my ulterior motives. Talk about feminine intuition.

"If you loved Wina," I said earnestly, "you would give it to me. She doesn't know what has happened to her second stepmother or her brother. You don't answer her letters. She must be out of her mind by now. I was and still am her only hope."

"Why should I believe you? Why should I trust you? Who are you? I don't know you. You are just another drunken customer I met at Mtalika View Bar."

I reached for my wallet, opened it, took out an aerogram, and gave it to her. She opened it and glanced up and down helplessly.

"You know I can't read or speak English."

"By the time this letter reaches you," I translated the relevant paragraph for her, "I really will have gone bonkers with worry …"

"But is it Wina's writing?" Shaibu interrupted maliciously.

"It's Wina's," Margaret answered him.

Someone heaved a sigh. We all looked at her expectantly.

"My baby." She started crying uncontrollably.

I got up and put my arm round her. "I'll take you home," I said quietly.

Her shoulders quivered as she got up, collected her bag, wiped her eyes, and walked unaided to the door. I waved goodbye to my newly found friends, as I followed Margaret.

"Are you still going to write the story?" I heard Shaibu ask in the hush that Margaret left behind.

"How could I," Jo replied, "after all that?"

"I knew you couldn't," Shaibu chortled. "That's the problem with story-tellers who learn their art by correspondence. They are always overwhelmed by technicalities of form and content. I can see him purring enthusiastically over his latest instalment of 'Story-writing in Ten Easy-to Follow Lessons'."

I shut the door behind me.

The Rubbish Dump

The boy squatted on the ground, bending over a small toy car. The bodywork consisted of rectangular pieces of cardboard inserted between a forest of bent pieces of wire. The wheels were empty boot polish tins and the steering rod was one long reed which culminated in a wheel from the top of a large baby powder tin.

The expression on the boy's face was a study in concentration: contracted mouth, wrinkled nose, furrowed brow, and slit eyes. His hands worked impatiently on short pieces of wire that had come loose in the chassis. After a moment he straightened up with a satisfied grunt, revved the engine, and burst into song:

Azungu nzeru
kupanga ndege
Sikanthu kena
koma ndi khama.

The shrill notes pierced the air and filled the civil service quarters for a few minutes. The song was interrupted by the squeak, rattle, thump of a wheelbarrow along the dust road twenty yards away from the last row of houses. The boy's song dangled in the air, faltered and fell. The squeak, rattle, thump increased steadily in volume as it approached.

It was Mazambezi. That's what everyone called him - behind his back. Mazambezi, the airport garbage collector, pushing his wheelbarrow.

The boy stopped maneuvering the car into the space between two broken bricks. His body went slack as he remembered that it was Friday and he had missed the big plane landing, coming from London. Locally they called it 'Four Engine'. Mazambezi was bringing in the rubbish from that plane, which meant it had landed hours ago. The boy cursed himself for having forgotten to be on the balcony to watch the passengers in their expensive clothes stepping down from the plane, carrying large bags, cameras, and all sorts of mysterious things from far off lands. It was now too late to run to the airport. The visitors would have been driven off to their various destinations by now. Even the out-going passengers would have boarded the plane.

The increasingly piercing whine of a plane about to take off confirmed this. The boy gazed at where he knew the plane would appear in the sky. A moment later, the corrugated iron roof tops rattled violently as the thundering roar threatened to tear them off. This was one disadvantage of living near an international airport. Every now and then the staff quarters were shattered by mini earthquakes caused by planes landing or taking off. Not that the boy minded. The noise filled him with an almost superstitious awe and reverence at the intelligence that could make those big things fly like that in the sky.

A few minutes later, the boy was straining his eyes to follow the silver streak overtaking and outstripping the clouds. After a moment or two, he could see it no longer. He wondered who would be on it today and where they would be going. His father had once told him that the plane stopped at such places as Salisbury and Johannesburg, before going on to England. When he could read he would have fun finding these places in the book his father had told him all the famous places on earth were written. Still, it was a pity he had not been on the balcony today.

The rumble of the wheelbarrow was very near now. It sounded like the feeble spluttering of an ancient motor cycle, too old to start, yet persisting in igniting for a few moments. The boy maneuvered his car between the two bricks and took the path that joined the road Mazambezi would take. The rubbish dump was only a hundred yards away from the house.

"Moni, Joey," the man greeted the boy.

"Moni." Joey stopped a few feet away to watch his progress.

"You haven't gone to school today?"

"We've got a month's holiday."

"That's good."

"What have you got this time?"

"I don't know," Mazambezi replied. "A few pieces of cheese mixed with vomit, maybe."

Joey crinkled his nose at the mention of vomit. Someone had told him once that the passengers on the plane sometimes vomitted in bags provided for that purpose. Joey wondered what made people vomit when flying in a plane. He had seen his father vomit in the house when drunk. It was not very nice.

Joey kept his distance and watched the old man push the antiquated machine in front of him. The machine seemed to be an extension of Mazambezi. Joey could not imagine him without it. Both had been one of the quaint scenes he had first noticed when his family had been transferred to this airport district.

The machine had once been a gleaming piece of metal like the shiny planes at the airport, but that must have been long ago, in the hardware shop. Now it was marked at irregular rusty intervals with layers of flattened dried out bits of what had once been cheese, tinned beef, and other non-descript things. It wore the indifferent color of a piece of metal dug up from damp earth after a long period. The wheel revolved round a worn out axle. This was where the agonizing squeak came from. Apparently, grease had been applied to stop it, but that, too, was years ago. Only blackened encrustations were left to commemorate the fact.

They made a pair, these two: the dry and wet seasons had left their marks on man and machine. The tattered clothes of the old man were more suitable for the pit than for wearing. Clearly visible in many places through the torn overalls were multi-colored – because of additional patches – khaki shorts. An equally ancient army jungle hat, pulled closely over the head, served as protection against the dry heat. The brim had a wide gash in it so that the headgear was more of a cap than anything else. The short black hair underneath was mixed with a lot of grey, giving it the color of sooty lime.

The rubbish pit made itself felt as they neared. Wave after wave of stench enveloped Joey and Mazambezi, and went on in its oppressive embrace to the native quarters.

Joey remembered the revulsion he had felt during the first days he had noticed Mazambezi's daily ritual. He had followed the old man after a week or two of suppressed curiosity. Joey had wondered what made the old man take so long at the rubbish pit after tipping his load. The odor had got thicker and more oppressive as he had crept nearer and nearer where the old man sat gazing into the pit. Joey's nostrils twitched violently as the offensive rush of foul air flowed into him, past him, until he felt as though he was swimming in liquid rot. It clawed at his throat and settled in his stomach. Nausea hit him. He stumbled over a projection and cried out as he fell onto some disgustingly soft, sticky substance. He shuddered at the contact, convulsed for a few moments, and wretched painfully. A hand fell on his shoulder as he tried to get to his feet.

"Are you all right?" The gruff voice of the old man seemed to come out of the ooze around him.

"Don't touch me!" he shouted. His face contorted, he sprawled back into the mess, instinctively recoiling from the other.

"I said, are you all right?"

"Don't come near me!" he yelled wrathfully. "You filthy, dirty, old Mazambezi!"

The old man straightened up slowly. Joey succeeded in his second attempt to get up, and sped off across the field that separated the pit from the houses. He glanced back once, from a safe distance, to see the old man settle back in the position he had found him. Well, Joey thought, at least he had satisfied his curiosity. The old man spent some time rummaging in the débris and salvaged left-over food from the load. This he piled onto a piece of paper and ate. In his blindness Joey had fallen onto the old man's picnic lunch. Joey looked at his begrimed clothes and wondered what the grey particles sticking there were. He remembered about vomiting in bags in airplanes and started sobbing. He went behind the kitchen to let his passion loose. His mother found him there. The clothes told their own story, and she reprimanded him severely for going to play at the rubbish pit. Didn't he know he could get all sorts of diseases from there? When this was reported to his father it earned Joey a thrashing. The adults had concluded he had joined Mazambezi at table.

After that incident, he spent his free time on the balcony at the airport watching the planes come and go. He got to know the timetable of scheduled flights and could tell what plane was due long before it was announced over the intercom. The other times were spent building his car, repairing it, and driving it around the house. He had built an intricate network of roads connecting the house to most of the important airports his father had told him about: Tokyo, Paris, London and New York. He stopped at each airport for Coca Cola or tea. After a time, he had grown tired of going there by road and had built a plane. The first attempt was a disaster. It squatted like a rotten lump of potato. The second attempt did not satisfy Joey either, but he nonetheless flew it to Moscow, Tokyo, London, New York, and back.

Mazambezi continued his rounds and Joey could not help meeting him sometimes, since New York airport was near the road which the garbage collector used. One day Joey was urgently trying to communicate to the man in the tower at the airport in Tokyo, in the manner his father had taught him: "Request permission to land," he intoned over and over again as he circled round: "Request permission to land. Can you hear me? Over."

"Look, Joey," a voice interrupted the pilot, "I've got a real plane for you."

It was Mazambezi. He had walked soundlessly from the pit without his wheelbarrow, and was holding out a miniature 'Air Rhodesia' to him. Joey looked fearfully at him. The brown eyes were almost apologetic. The boy backed a step, his mouth working. He glanced at his home, grabbed the plane and ran as fast as he could to behind the kitchen. There he knelt down and held the plane to his chest, and panted for a few minutes. There were tears in his eyes as, after a time, he looked about him again. The old man was gone. Joey had not heard the wheelbarrow grinding off. He stood up and peeked around the corner of the kitchen. He pulled back and put the plane under his shirt. It made a bulge that would not deceive anyone. Joey quickly crossed his arms where the bulges were most pronounced. With a palpitating heart, he started shaking his shoulders ostentatiously, all the while walking towards the house, singing:

> *Azungu nzeru*
> *kupanga ndege*
> *Sikanthu kena*
> *koma ndi khama.*

Luckily his mother was cleaning the main bedroom. Joey ran to the little room where he slept. He found his school bag with some exercise books in it and hid 'Air Rhodesia' there. Among the school books were an odd assortment of foreign coins, tourist guides, empty cigarette packets and so on, collected from the airport. Every time he went to the balcony he came back with one or two items to add to his treasure. During the holidays, it was easy to hide them there. No one would think of looking for anything in his bag.

Joey unrolled his sleeping mat and lay down. He listened to his mother cleaning. His arm stole to the bag and came out with the plane. He inspected it carefully. It had a broken tail, but if he held it where the tail should have been it would pass as an airworthy craft.

"Joey! Are you in there?"

"Yes, mother," Joey answered, precipitately shoving the plane into the bag and pushing it back against the wall. When the door opened he was breathing heavily on the mat.

"What are you doing down there?" His mother's imposing frame filled the doorway.

"I … I have a headache, mother."

"Why didn't you tell me."

"You were busy, mother."

"Too busy to tell me you are ill?"

"I … I …"

"Come here, Joey."

"Yes, mother."

"Now, I won't have you pretending you're sick." The inevitable finger was two inches away from his nose.

"No, mother."

"I saw you running about and singing not a few minutes ago."

"I … I … mother …"

"Don't lie to me."

"No, mother."

"Good. Now, I want you to go to the grocery to get me a pound of sugar and a packet of tea leaves."

"Yes, mother."

"Here's the money."

Joey took the money without a word and went out, worried. What if his mother found the plane? He sped to the grocery and was back in record time. His mother met him with:

"I thought you had a terrible headache?"

"I … I. It's gone, mother."

"Good. Now, help me move these things so that I can clean your room. Do you have to be so messy?"

Joey ran to the school bag and held it tightly against him.

"I said everything, not only your bag."

"Yes, mother."

Joey put the bag gingerly on top of his other books, clothes and mat, and went out of the room. He put them in a corner and stood guard over them. Moments later, his mother called out to him that she had finished. Another careful operation took the objects back to his room.

"You're acting very strangely." His mother was looking hard at him. "Are you sure your headache is gone?"

"No, mother." Joey avoided looking at his mother. "It's come back."

"Maybe," she said. "You can lie down."

Joey unrolled his mat again and lay down. He felt calmer now. His father came home late that night, drunk again and singing, "For he's a jolly good fellow and so say all of me." Joey listened as he noisily asked for his supper. His mother's voice came faintly to Joey's ears at intervals as his father explained loudly that a white man had bought him the drinks. The white man was a nice man, he proclaimed, for – it was his favorite question —where would the black man be without him? When he was in that mood he could be tedious. He would go on enumerating the good things the white man had brought to the country: jobs, cars, airplanes, not to mention booze. Joey fell asleep as the voice droned on about Africans, who should be eternally grateful, now living in decent houses, wearing decent clothes, and leading decent lives. His mother had retired to the bedroom, although he knew she was listening. His father spoke for all the world to hear.

It took Joey a week to muster enough courage to go and meet Mazambezi on the road. He thanked him shyly for the plane, but the old man grunted something that was drowned in the rattle, squeak, thump of the wheelbarrow. Joey followed hesitantly behind the two. The old man's cracked feet made little eddies of dust as he trudged on. The overalls were as soiled as the machine. Joey quickened his steps to walk alongside Mazambezi.

"What have you got this time?"

"I don't know." The old man was looking straight ahead of him. "A few lumps of meat with the usual mixture."

Joey was careful not to crinkle his face. The man and the boy turned into the path that led to the rubbish dump. The nauseous smell got stronger as they got nearer.

The pit was very old and large, but shallow. It had been there long before Joey was born. The original rubbish had putrified enough to turn into earth underneath. It was not Mazambezi alone who used the place. The civil servants also did. It abounded in greying pieces of *nsima* scraped from the bottoms of pots, yellows and greens of banana, pawpaw and orange peel, chaff of sugar cane or maize, not to mention baby, chicken, and dog shit. Every imaginable kind of waste matter found its way to the pit. The fresh rubbish, the insides of chicken and guts of fish, were feasts for bloated bluebottles. They and the fruit flies buzzed angrily like bees, when the man and the boy reached the mouth of the pit. The crows circled above them, cawing noisily. Other forms of life bred in the empty milk, fish, and beef tins strewn about in the pit.

"Did all that come from the plane?"

"Yes."

"They must eat a lot."

"When the white man eats, he eats."

"It's not only the white man who travels in planes."

"No. But still it's white man's food. You don't see *khobwe* or *mgaiwa* in the wheelbarrow, do you?"

"No. What do the Wenela people eat?"

"Bread."

"Oh?"

"Just imagine." Mazambezi was all of a sudden talkative. He had stopped the wheelbarrow at the edge of the pit and picked out a tin from its depths. "Just imagine," he repeated vehemently. "Where do you think this tin came from?"

"London?"

"No."

"Paris?"

"No. It was made in Hong Kong," he announced triumphantly. "I sit here every day and look into the pit. I pick up bits of paper or beef cans and look at them and imagine where they came from. Japan? Russia? England? America? South Africa? As I sit here munching bits of cheese, a whole world is opened up to me. How many thousands of miles has this tin of fish travelled? What places has this empty packet of biscuits visited? What person vomited into this bag? What language does he speak? What hopes and dreams does he have? I don't need to ride in their planes. As I sit here Russia, America, Hong Kong, England are in my grasp. They all find their way into this rubbish dump -"

"I do the same," Joey interrupted, "when I go to the balcony to watch the planes come and go. Every day at school as I open my books I wonder if I will ever be educated enough to read more about these places. Even visit them. Just imagine being able to walk in the streets of London or New York or Tokyo!"

"I know how you feel." Mazambezi had a faraway expression on his face as he looked at the boy beside him.

"But I've also seen the places." Joey's face lit up.

"Have you?"

"Yes. Every day when I drive my car, or the plane you gave me, I see them so clearly. I drink Coca Cola in New York, have tea in London, and go for a drive in Tokyo."

They sat at the edge of the dump, legs dangling in the pit, and looked at the broken bottles made in England, or squashed food cans made in U.S.A. and plastic odds and ends made in Japan or Russia. Each was lost in his own thoughts. Humid putrefaction wafted around them, into them, and through them to the native quarters. The crows circled above them like black planes about to land. In the dump, the yellow, grey and brown flies also circled and dived into juicy offal.

"Here," the old man interrupted their dreams. "Have a piece of cheese. Maybe it came from South Africa."

Joey stretched out a hand. He had decided to lean against the wheelbarrow for more comfort. He chewed the stale cheese silently watching the antics of the flies on a pool of vomit. The buzzing of the flies and the cries of the crows seemed to be the only sounds but this was interrupted by the rising cadences of a plane starting.

"It's the 'Four Engine'," Joey remarked.

"Yes, it's the big plane taking off."

"I wonder if it will stop in Salisbury."

"Maybe."

"I wonder who is in it."

"Oh, the usual. Rich fat white men, brown men and a few blacks."

"Students going for more education."

"Yes, I forgot about those." Mazambezi stood up with a grunt and wiped calloused hands on his overalls. "I've got to be going too."

"Goodbye," Joey said slowly. He straightened up from the wheelbarrow.

"We'll be meeting again tomorrow?"

"Yes." The old man lifted the bars of the machine. In a few minutes the squeak, rattle, thump faded in the distance. Joey wondered who would die first - the man or the machine. The rattle, squeak, thump of the machine and the stoic silence of the man behind it had the same quality as the mournful hoot of an owl. But Joey knew that the daily exchange of "What has the big plane brought today?" - "Oh, bits and pieces from the whiteman's land." would continue for some time yet. The left-overs, garbage and whatever would keep finding their way to the waiting rubbish dump; the flies and crows; Mazambezi and Joey.

Go Back to Your Room

Ndaziona's elbows ached from the prolonged contact with the wooden table top. The first joints of his middle finger, forefinger, and thumb were cramped from the extended gripping of the multi-cornered plastic ballpoint pen. He felt as if the outer side of his little finger had been rubbed thin from moving too closely and too often on the smooth pages of his exercise books. Ndaziona had been doing his homework—History, Biology, English, with more to do—for almost three hours now. He felt the strain on the other parts of his body too: neck, back, buttocks, and thigh muscles. It had taken him longer to work on some parts due to the periodic bursts of conversation between his grandfather and mother in the next room.

Akunjila, his grandfather, had landed on them from the village that afternoon. His mother knew what his father, who was away then, would have done had he been around to do the entertaining: bought him a liter of *kachasu*, the home distilled gin. Akunjila approved of this gesture as soon as he saw his grandson plonk the tall bottle on the table in the sitting room. A short squat glass accompanied it. Ndaziona poured some of the pale faint yellow fluid into the glass. The fumes wafted up to his bent face, stinging his mouth, nose and eyes. They swirled into his lungs and he almost choked as he turned away to offer his grandfather the first drink for that day.

"May our forefathers be blessed," Akunjila intoned. "This is hospitality at its best."

Kachasu, Ndaziona had been told, was the only effective drink for the octagenarian. He regarded any other alcohol—bottled beer, maize beer, or the packeted stuff—as women's or children's drink. When he resorted to them, which was rare and under extreme pressure, he still mixed them with the hard stuff.

"This is entirely unacceptable," Akunjila complained in the next room when his daughter-in-law came to collect something. He seemed to have reached the early stages of inebriation. "I can't drink alone like this."

"I'm preparing supper in the kitchen," his mother said, "so I can't sit and chat with you all the time."

"I don't mean you," Akunjila almost snorted. "You don't drink."

"Your son comes home late especially at the weekends," was the apologetic reply.

"I can't wait for him all night. Besides, the bottle is almost gone. Is there another one?"

"We bought only one."

"Are you sending the boy for another one?"

This was what Ndaziona dreaded: having to be sent for refills or replacements. His mother saved him.

"It's rather late, and not safe for him to go back to the township for more. Besides, you know what happened to him the last time you were here."

"I could go with him."

"There are a lot of drunks and thugs out there. They go about molesting kids, old women and men."

"It's all right, my daughter. You're doing enough to look after me. It's just that I came to visit my son, and what do I find?"

"He didn't know you were coming and he had no reason to stay at home. You know your son … "

"Of course, I know my son," Akunjila chuckled. "Who else knows him better than I do?"

Ndaziona could not concentrate on the Math he was working on. He dreaded to think what it would be like to eat supper alone with his grandfather in such a state. He looked at the textbook and the hieroglyphs he had made on the page of his exercise book. His gaze wandered over the table to the other textbooks and exercise books in two separate piles. The Math set box, ruler, rubber, and pencil were in the middle.

***

Ndaziona's room was the converted store of the two-roomed house. There were cartons, baskets, and mats shoved to one side of the room. A concrete slab, shoulder-high, was midway between the floor and the roof on one side of the wall. He used the slab as a shelf for his other books, the suitcase of clothes he was not currently using, and more cartons of knicknacks he had accumulated over the years: torches, batteries, pieces of wire, catapults, pebbles, shells, and the like. The other length of the wall was occupied by a single bed, above which he had pasted posters of pop singers, soccer stars, and athletes. There were also pictures of pen pals he corresponded with from England, Europe, USA, and even Japan and China. It was greater fun writing to them than doing his homework or entertaining a drunken grandfather.

The table Ndaziona was working on was pushed against the width of the wall between the bed and the concrete slab. During the day, the gloom of the room was alleviated by the light coming from the small three-paned window. The window overlooked the garden and the grass and trees outside. Ndaziona had been working in his room after cleaning, washing, and ironing. He had looked up to see his grandfather approaching from the road connecting the staff quarters to the main road. His look held dismay, if not dread and resentment, at the visitor advancing toward the house. He harbored all these emotions because something always happened when his grandfather came visiting. Akunjila's last visit to town had almost been fatal.

His mother had sent him, as usual, to buy a bottle of *kachasu* from his father's favorite distiller. The township was about three kilometers away, and he used his father's bicycle. Since Ndaziona was small and short, he could not ride the bicycle on the crossbar and use the saddle on top. He peddled the adult bicycle by pushing his legs between the three bars instead. On the return trip, he coasted down a slope at greater speed than usual. He lost control of the bicycle. The handlebars moved to and fro on the steep slope and the next moment he found himself on the embankment amidst broken grass, twigs, and churned earth. He must have passed out because he suddenly found several hands of women on him and the bicycle. They lifted both of them, boy and machine, uttering sympathetic noises.

"He's too young to ride that bike," one of them said.

"You shouldn't ride it again," another admonished, "or else you'll fall off again."

"Just walk it home," a third concluded.

Ndaziona righted himself, walked the bicycle a few meters and then ignored the women's advice.

On reaching home he parked the bicycle against the wall dividing the main house from the outhouses. He went into the kitchen and emerged with a cup of water. He sat against the outside wall to clean his wound. There was a three-inch gash on the inside of his right thigh, where the bottom bicycle pump hook had torn at him when he fell off. Fortunately there was not much blood coming out.

"*Mwana wanga!*" his mother wailed as she came out to investigate what had happened to the errand boy.

"Look!" Akunjila had come out, too. "The boy is hurt!"

It was the first time he had cried since he had turned teenager. They had taken him to the clinic. He had come back with several stitches on his thigh.

It was also with curiosity that Ndaziona watched the progress of the frail bent frame of his grandfather. He looked so out of place in his floppy, frayed black trousers and long khaki shirt hanging out. He tapped his way past the row of four houses to theirs, the last one. It was only then that Ndaziona was galvanized into action.

"Mother!" he shouted. "Grandfather is here!"

He ran out of his room past the sitting-cum-dining room to the front door. He found Akunjila's bent form at the bottom of the steps. He had a small bundle in the other hand.

"Grandfather!" he went down the steps "Let me carry that!" He reached out for the bundle and proffered the other hand to help the visitor up the steps.

"May the spirits of the forefathers be blessed," Akunjila breathed. "How you have grown. Is your father home?"

"Not yet. It's Saturday so he won't come home till late."

"Still drinking heavily, is he? I thought he nearly died when he fell off the bicycle on one of his binges?"

His father's accident had nothing to do with Akunjila's visit. Ndaziona only knew about it the following morning, when he saw his mother helping her husband go painfully to the bathroom and staying there to bathe his wounds. His father could hardly wash himself or walk about. He could not hold a pen between his swollen fingers. He was given sick leave for a fortnight or so. Ndaziona got only fragments of what had really happened: A bicycle accident could not have caused the kinds of bruises, cuts, and wounds his father brought home that night. There was a woman involved, and it was a rival that had got together a gang to dissuade his father from continuing the affair.

"At least your mother is here," it was a statement. Ndaziona assented as they finished climbing the steps to the *khonde* and went into the house.

"Mother!" he announced again unnecessarily. "Grandfather is here."

"I'm coming!" came from the outhouses at the back. Grandfather tapped his way to a seat and fell rather than sat down in it.

If a equals ten, b equals fifteen, and c ... it was not as if Akunjila was always associated with misfortunes. Some of his visits were uneventful. In actual fact, there was a good side to them: he always brought something from his garden: bananas, groundnuts, pears, sugarcane. Things Ndaziona could boast about to his schoolmates, especially to Nkhutukumve, the bully, and his gang. Things other people had to buy in town. They were home-grown and freely given. Yet much as he itched to, Ndaziona could not open the bundle Akunjila had brought that afternoon to find out what grandfather had brought this time. It was the privilege of the adults to do that. There would be a special ritual for the gift presentation. It would be considered an impertinence if he did open it. *Find the value of y* ...

"Ndaziona!" his mother called out to him.

"Ndazi ...!" his grandfather echoed impatiently. "Your mother is calling you. Why don't you answer?"

He had heard his mother, first time. His mother knew it, too. She had done so several times a day, ever since he could remember. Akunjila's previous visits had witnessed similar calls. His grandfather knew it, too. The dividing door was too thin to keep out even normal conversation at any time. That's how he knew of his parents' numerous quarrels and fights, yes, even fights. He knew quite a lot from his room.

"I'm coming!" He left the books open on the table.

"Why are you hiding?" Akunjila confronted him between sips of *kachasu*, as the boy passed him. "What is it you do in there?"

"Homework. I told you that before."

"You're just avoiding your grandfather. That's what. Like your father. I wrote to him that I was coming today. I don't come here often enough, yet everyone is running away from me."

"You know I enjoy having you around, grandfather," he said, before opening the back door. "All those stories you tell me when you come ..."

He opened the door and descended the back steps. The outhouses consisted of kitchen, bathroom, toilet, and pantry.

He joined his mother in the kitchen. The only illumination was the open wood fire in the middle of three firestones in one corner. His mother was sitting on a low stool. Beside her were plates of *nsima* and *ndiwo*: hers to eat in the kitchen and the visitor's to share with Ndaziona.

"Take these to your grandfather."

He reached down for the covered plates and placed them one pair on top of the other, for a single trip. He had left the back door open to ease his re-entry.

"Here's the food at last."

Ndaziona did not answer. He went back to the kitchen for the washbasin. He found his grandfather already at the table. He had uncovered the plates.

"I love dried *mlamba*," Akunjila commented. Ndaziona did not answer. He pulled out his own chair and held out the water for the old man to wash his hands first.

"Dried fish goes well with *kachasu*." Akunjila looked at the peppered open *mlamba* on the plate. For a moment, Ndaziona thought the old man would start drooling. He sat down and they attacked the food without any preambles.

"This is why I enjoy coming to town." Akunjila cut off a chunk of fish from the tail end. He chomped on it. Ndaziona wondered how many teeth the octagenarian had left. "In the village there is only pumpkin leaves today, cassava leaves yesterday, and potato leaves tomorrow. Leaves, leaves, leaves, every day."

"I thought there's fish in Mzimundilinde River?"

"Gone, all gone, not even *matemba* left," he shook his head, and then a sparkle came to his eyes. "Do you know it was your father who dug the

channel from Mzimundilinde right into and past the village to irrigate the
dimbas?"

"Did he?" Ndaziona remembered the channel. It was almost half a
kilometer long from and to the big river, making a big curve to
encompass the village and water its gardens, right on their doorsteps, so
it seemed. What a feat!

"He didn't tell you that? That was all his doing. Single-handed. Not
his useless elder brother. All Ndilekeni did was brag about this or that
but with nothing to show for it."

"Where's Uncle Ndilekeni now?"

"Back in his wife's village. That's where he built his house. He left no
mark in his own village. At least your father had the stream, it's more
than just a channel: it never goes dry. Even at the height of summer it
trickles on heroically. That's it, heroically, like your father. You know,
your uncle and father actually fought by that stream one time."

"Did they? Why?"

"Just childish quarrels. It must have been over a girl. That's what
Ndilekeni was always boasting about. It was quite a bloody fight, I tell
you, with almost anything that came by: sticks, stones, legs, and all."

"Who won?"

"Your father, of course, although the younger of the two. Do you
think anyone can beat your father?"

Ndaziona nearly choked on his food. He looked around the table and
realized that he had forgotten to bring the drinking water. He excused
himself and went out hastily.

The first and last time he saw his father in a fight had not
demonstrated any heroism in him at all. On one of those rare occasions
he had drunk at home, he invited his friends. They were at it from
afternoon through supper to mid-evening. Since Ndaziona's room was
just beyond the sitting-cum-dining room, it meant that he went past the
revelries periodically. It was bearable in the afternoon: he could play or
work outside on the *khonde*. He went away to the shops and returned
before dark. It was different in the evening. After supper he could not
work or sleep in his room, as the festivities grew louder and even angrier.
They were brought to a stop by a clatter of chairs and bottles. There was

the sound of a scuffle and a falling body. Ndaziona darted out of his room to find his father sitting down dazedly on the floor. The two other men were holding Mr Ndakulapa, their neighbor, restraining him from continuing the fight.

"Go back to your room!" snarled his father, when he saw Ndaziona.

Ndaziona shut the door quickly behind him. He was angry and embarrassed as he sat back at the writing table. His father had looked so stupefied, even so childish as he sat there on the floor trying to get up. It was like the time Nkhutukumve had knocked Ndaziona down on the school playground, with the gang holding the bully back.

"Here's some drinking water, grandfather." Ndaziona came back with the glasses and placed one in front of the other.

"Drink water? Who? How can I drink water when I have that?"

The *kachasu* bottle was still on the little table by the settee, where the old man had sat the whole afternoon. It was now just below half. There was some in the glass, too. The old man must have been taking it easy. Perhaps he hoped his son would come back soon to join him. Ndaziona wondered at what stage in the bottle's drainage the drinker would be too drunk to continue. Like Akunjila, his father never knew when to stop if he was angry at something or with somebody.

The night of the fight, Ndaziona's father was not only angry at somebody, he was jealous. He had always suspected Ndakulapa of having an affair with his mother. Ndaziona had caught fragments of exchanges between his parents at different times. The angry words between the men on the night of the fight only confirmed this. Even when the visitors had left, his father continued drinking. Ndaziona must have been asleep for some time when he heard a crash that seemed to shake the whole building.

"Amayo!" A cry from his mother. Ndaziona jumped out of bed and opened his door just as his mother rushed out of the bedroom. She collapsed in one of the chairs, holding her forehead tightly with both hands. There was blood spurting out between the fingers, reddening the knuckles, wrists, arms, and dripping on her clothes. Ndaziona ran to her and stopped. He looked down at his mother waving her head back and forth, her eyes closed tight, her face proclaiming silent agony. There was a two-inch gash on her forehead. Ndaziona did not know what to do. He felt faint.

"Go back to your room!" His father stormed out of the bedroom.

Ndaziona whimpered and backed out of the room, looking at his father, then mother, father, mother. The last vision he had was his father towering over his cowering mother. Ndaziona's head swam. He nearly threw up. He did not sleep that night.

The following morning his mother's head was in bandages.

"He pushed me against the cupboard. The corner ...." That was all the explanation he was given. At least, his father had taken her to the clinic in the night. Yet the following morning, he was not there to face her. It was Ndaziona who saw and felt the great pain she was in. She could hardly see. Squinting pulled at the stitches, causing fresh blood flows. Ndaziona helped her in the kitchen and in the house.

"Your father was really a man." Akunjila was washing his hands. The fish and nearly all the bones were gone from the plate. "At your age he was already fighting for his women. He wouldn't let anyone, even his brother, touch his woman."

Ndaziona was confused: he piled the plates on top of each other regardless of which could fit where. He washed his hands, as his grandfather groped his way back to the easy chair. He reached for the bottle and poured himself some more.

"This is good." He took a sip. "Do you know when your father started drinking?"

Ndaziona felt like bolting out of the room. He picked up the plates instead, shakily.

"At your age, actually." Akunjila answered his own question. "That's it. It made a man out of him."

Ndaziona dashed out of the room.

"What's the matter?" His mother peered at him from the gloom of the kitchen fire. She, too, had finished eating.

"Nothing," he almost sobbed. "I ... I think grandfather is drunk."

"Don't mind him. The Mwaonekeras are all alike. Him and his son."

"I don't want to be like them." Ndaziona almost screamed into the night.

"Of course not. You're different. People say you take after me. Why, you're both son and daughter to me."

That was it: daughter. Ndaziona, like his mother, had always wanted a sister to care for, to watch growing up, to play with at home, or to take to school, but no one came after him.

His mother never talked about it afterward, but she had been pregnant at least once, as far as Ndaziona could remember. During her pregnancy, she joked about the little sister who was coming to join them soon. She did not mention a little brother. She grew bigger. Then it happened. A cry in the night. A night trip to the hospital. Several weeks in hospital. She had lost the little sister. Ndaziona knew why: his father had hit her in the stomach in one of his drunken moods.

"It's not mine," he had heard him growl on the night of the hospital. Then the piercing scream.

"Go back to your room!" his father had snarled at him, when Ndaziona peeked out. He cowered back and bolted the door, trembling and sobbing uncontrollably.

Ndaziona was told the following day that he could not see his mother for several days. When he did, he joined his mother in weeping. Back in his room, he could not hold back the tears the whole day and night.

He cooked, cleaned, and looked after his father, while his mother was in hospital. His father was as uncommunicative and sullen as ever. He growled and snarled his wishes at Ndaziona. Ndaziona kept to his room in between chores. Mute. Terrified of his father's fury, now that the other victim was out of the house. One wrong step or word and he would break just about every one of his bones.

"Your father took after me," Akunjila chuckled in his seat. "I, too, was drinking at your age."

Ndaziona had finished clearing the table of the washbasin and the drinking glasses. He was going back to his room.

"Now, be sociable." Akunjila's voice was slurred. "Don't leave me alone again. Come and sit here. I will tell you the other adventures your father had growing up."

"I haven't finished my homework."

"There's tomorrow."

"I go to church in the morning. And I have soccer at school in the afternoon."

"I want to make a man out of you." Akunjila quavered and gestured to the bottle. "Come, finish that. There's only one shot left. That's good enough for a start."

"No, grandfather." Ndaziona was shaking again. "I'm too young to drink."

Ndaziona could hear Nkhutukumve, the class bully and his gang boasting how drunk they were at the disco last Saturday afternoon. If Ndaziona complied with Akunjila's invitation, he could join his classmates boasting about their weekend sprees. He would be a hero, too. The gang would begin to respect him, then. Perhaps they would let him play with them, too, smoking even. Nkhutukumve and his mates smoked other things, too, not just tobacco. If he joined them …

Perhaps he should accept Akunjila's invitation, and let his father find him stupidly drunk. Ndaziona would beat him at his own game. He would turn the tables round. His father would mend his ways and would stay at home and care for his family. Perhaps his father would then stop beating his mother, and she would have a baby girl for him to play with. Perhaps they would then be a loving family together.

His father was not entirely cruel: he took his wife to the hospital after beating her up. His mother might not have been entirely demonstrative either, but she had not run away from her wife-beating husband. On the contrary, she stuck it out; she had even nursed her husband after his bicycle accident. Sometimes, his father brought Ndaziona some magazines and books from his workplace, for his son to read. Ndaziona had put them on the slab of concrete in his room, as part of his growing library. His father's additions made more delightful reading than the dreadfully boring textbooks surrounding him, threatening to drown him in his own room.

***

Perhaps, given a chance, they could renew their loving ways. His father had once started teaching his wife how to ride the bicycle. Ndaziona had always trailed behind them during the rides. They had stopped the lessons because his mother had developed swellings between her legs after a few days. It was not his father's fault that they stopped the riding lessons. Then again, his father allowed him to ride the bicycle on his own. It was not his father's fault that Ndaziona fell off it once. There must be something they could go back to and start all over again, as a loving and caring family.

No, his father would not beat him. Why should he? It was Akunjila, his own father, who said that he wanted to initiate him into the ways of the adults. Akunjila would even take his side: you, too, started drinking at Ndaziona's age, he would reiterate. I, too, started drinking at your son's age. So what's new? What's wrong with the boy taking after us?

No, no, his father was too much of a bully to see the logic in that. He would beat Ndaziona from room to room into the garden and beyond, till he could not stand up straight anymore. Ndaziona would end up like his mother: several weeks in hospital. Ndaziona could feel the sweat wetting his armpits, although his teeth chattered as if chilled. A sob he wanted to stifle started building up under his chest. He ran to his room before it exploded in front of his grandfather.

"Coward! You're no better than a girl, really." The words were flung at him from the octagenarian. They ricochetted on the closing door as Ndaziona bolted it behind him. He trembled in front of the writing table. That's what Nkhutukumve and his gang called him at school. His knees melted under him. He supported himself with the back of the chair as he sat down. He had planned to do Bible Knowledge before going to bed, and to prepare himself for church the following day. He looked at the piles of textbooks, notebooks, and other school materials. No more than a sissy, really, they seemed to jeer at him. He groped for the Bible under one pile of books. As he opened it randomly, tears blurred his vision. His mind did a kaleidoscopic swirl: *for God so loved the world he sent his only grandfather ... Birimankhwe maso adatupa ninji ... change the following sentences into the passive ... when angle C is produced to D ... ababa apha bakha bakha wapha ababa ...*

Another Day at the Office

He joined the throng of people at the top of the small street leading from the market place. The main road marked the central artery of the main stream of people. They formed a vague column of marching feet kept in line by the fact that where the shops did not prevent them from leaving the main column, the ditches or the embankment did so further down.

A quarter to seven. Plenty of time. From the shop at the corner, the street leading from the market place to the office would only take fifteen minutes using Adam's mode of transport. The bells and the whirl of bicycle chains sounded a quicker form of locomotion which kept to the edges of the tarmac. This ensured that they were not directly in the path of the four-wheeled monsters that were the owners of that black road. But sometimes the cyclists violated this truth, only to be rudely reminded by the horn of an irate motorist and an oath that tore past at fifty miles per hour to leave the culprit shivering from its passage.

His faded, size seven brown shoes pinched a little after turning the corner. As traffic was heavier here on the main road, he was forced to keep to the pedestrian path. The dust formed a fine film over the polish his wife had applied that morning, as he was hurriedly washing his face and gargling his mouth to get on the road in time. The shoe repairer who worked opposite the vegetable stall in the market place had remarked in a friendly manner, "Why don't you let me keep this pair for patches on other customers' shoes? Another repair job on them and the makers won't recognize their handiwork."

He had muttered something to the effect that he did not see anything remarkable in the shoes. Just because he wanted another patch added to the areas where they pinched most did not warrant that he should turn into a charitable institution. Did he want him to go bare-footed to the office? Still, the man had done a good job. It would be another two months of daily wear before the customary slight limp reappeared.

The familiar face he met at the top of the street leading from the market place had greeted him amiably enough, "How are you this morning, Chingaipe?"

All he got in reply was the most overused cliché in the Civil Service—"Fifty-fifty"—which could be understood to mean anything from "I'm broke" to "I've got the grandfather of all hangovers." After that, Chingaipe did not show any signs of interest in developing the theme. The familiar face continued on its way, silently falling in behind Chingaipe.

The street leading from the market place was flanked by the Indian shops. Old structures built in a random, absent-minded fashion. Garish colors and dusty spaces sprinkled with wild grass. But as soon as you turned the corner at the top, you met the shops that made a pretense at being modern: cemented car parks for the customers, wide shop windows boasting imported merchandise. Chingaipe did not glance at them. His vision always centered on a spot vaguely ten feet in front of him.

The sound of water forming the background to the hum of engines, whirl of bicycle chains, and voices informed him he had left the shops far behind and was nearing the bridge over the small river they called Mzimundilinde. This receded as he climbed the long hill, still in the column of other workers heading for duties.

It usually took only fifteen minutes to walk from the top of the street leading from the market place to the office. Chingaipe noted subconsciously that he must have used ten minutes already, for the column of which he formed a part was now noticeably thicker and faster-moving. The October sun was already making itself felt. He traced the course of a trickle of sweat from his armpit along his ribs down to where his vest, shirt, underwear constricted him round his waist on account of the leather belt he used to keep his trousers up. The trickle down his thighs was from a different source altogether.

Chingaipe had dressed with his usual care. In spite of the hurry in the morning, he had looked at himself in the mirror to see that the parting on top of his head followed the usual groove. The spiked bamboo comb he used for this purpose never failed him. He could perform this action

71

in the dark if the need arose. The small knot on the cotton tie had been slightly to the left. He had pulled it right and shouted to his wife, Nambewe, in the kitchen, that he was off. Apparently, she had not heard him. The children, who were preparing to go to school, were making too much noise.

The road rose steeply after the river. Chingaipe felt the tie round his neck also constrict him, but he did not loosen the knot. The Higher Clerical Officer would give him a cold, disapproving stare if he noticed something faulty in the appearance of his clothes. Chingaipe's cheeks puffed a little and he breathed with some difficulty as he trundled up the steep incline. Only fifty yards to go.

He checked a little as he turned into the drive that led to the department he worked in. It was a huge, sprawling building that had belonged to some top government official in the pre-independence days. With the shortage of offices, the government had converted the residence into a block of offices, without changing the original design or the gardens surrounding it. The green corrugated iron roof was also the same. If you wanted to use the front door, you climbed the steps and came to a short passageway that led to what used to be the drawing room. It was now used by half-a-dozen young clerks, fresh from their School Certificate. Chingaipe's desk occupied one corner of this room.

The smaller path led to the back of the house—now office. You went through a bewildering maze of little rooms, including the bathroom and toilet, before you came to the same drawing room—now office—where Chingaipe had his desk.

Chingaipe took the smaller path to the back door. He always used the back door to his office, and every morning the Higher Clerical Officer's short but effective speech came to his mind: "Mr. Thomson has approached me about having a word with you lot in this room. Miss Prim, his secretary, has complained that, each time you clerks pass her desk by the front door in the next office, you stare at her. She doesn't like the way you look at her. Where are your manners, you people? Have you never seen a white lady before in your lives? Why do you have to gape at her each time you walk past her desk? Imagine all six, no, seven, of you marching past with eyes on her. What do you think she feels with fourteen eyes piercing her? You should be ashamed of yourselves. From now on, all junior clerks, typists, messengers, and telephone operators must use the back door to get to this room. That's not all. The toilet and bathroom on the other side of this room are closed to all junior staff. You're to use the toilets in the servants' quarters at the back of the house. I don't want to hear any more of this nonsense. Is that clear to everybody? I am going to write a memo to that effect right now. Copy to Mr. Thomson, one to Miss Prim, and a third to be pinned on that notice board to remind all of you."

Chingaipe opened the back door. It was seven o'clock. It seemed the only people around were the messengers and laborers. The rooms were so quiet. Even the girl who operated the switchboard had not yet made her appearance.

It was cooler inside. Chingaipe breathed a little easier. He passed the Executive Officer's office. The next one was the Higher Clerical Officer's. Both had originally been bedrooms. The drip, drip, drip was from the bathroom.

Chingaipe opened the door to the lounge—now office. It too was empty. He crossed the room to the far corner where his desk stood. He opened the window nearest to him and sat down with a sigh. He eased his feet a little out of the shoes to rest them. He dared not take them off all the way—the Higher Clerical Officer might walk in suddenly and find him in his holey socks.

He took the plastic cover off the typewriter, folded it carefully, pulled open the bottom right-hand drawer, laid it on the top of the papers there, and pushed the drawer shut. The keys stared blankly at him. He glanced at the two trays on the desk. The "IN" tray looked as full as it had been yesterday morning, the day before yesterday, last week, last month. It never seemed to be empty. The only empty one was the "OUT" tray.

Chingaipe put his hands on the desk, looked at his fingers for a brief moment, and pulled the top right-hand drawer open. He felt inside for what he wanted, and his hand came out with a razor blade. He proceeded to cut his nails slowly, piling the bits in the ashtray in front of him.

The other clerks found him sharpening a pencil, and to their enquiries about his state of health he said, without turning (he faced the window with his back to the room), "Half-half."

He recognized the individuals behind each voice and his tone of voice reflected how he felt about each of them. The six "Half-half's" varied slightly in their lukewarm nature. He felt rather out-of-place in this room. They were all products of secondary school, compared to his old Standard Three, taken twenty years ago. They must have thought him a bit odd too. Him with his slight limp, tight jacket, and baggy trousers, banging away like a thing possessed at an equally battered typewriter amidst their loud talk and sometimes lewd jokes.

Chingaipe looked up and noticed that the laborers outside had started work. That meant that the Higher Clerical Officer was coming. He opened the top file from the "IN" tray, took out a rough draft, and laid it on top. He pulled open the top left-hand drawer and took out three blank sheets of typing paper. He shut it, pulled open the drawer beneath, and counted two sheets of carbon paper, which he put between the typing paper. He shut the drawer and inserted all the sheets into the machine. He set the typewriter margins and began to type:

"Dear Sir,

With reference to your communication dated ... "

He could not type as fast as Miss Prim. There had been a time when he could have competed with her and not come off the worse. What did she type for Mr. Thomson which he didn't or couldn't anyway? Her with her superior secretarial airs. She was just a wisp of a woman really. Short, thin, almost angular. Long nose, thin lips. No bosom, no buttocks, no meat. Did she really think the young African clerks had any designs upon her? They might be fresh, but they knew there was no juice from that quarter. If it had been the telephone operator ... Now she was altogether different. The type that they really would turn and look at. Not that they had not, but they had come to grief. They were no match for her. That girl could be rude. He remembered the time he had been ready to go for the lunch break. She had preceded him into the passage with a friend. She had been speaking Yao so he could not understand, or so she had thought.

"At four o'clock, Chingaipe will knock off," she announced. "Hurry to his wife. Mrs. Chingaipe will stop pounding maize and hurry to the kitchen. She'll prepare food for the tired husband who is a copy-typist in a big government office. Ha! Ha! Ha!"

The girl had not realized how close to the truth she had been. Chingaipe paused in his typing. Neither had she realized how it had cut him to the core to be dissected and classified as she had done. True, his wife prepared food for him as soon as he reached home after work. Only because he did not go for lunch like the Executive Officer, like Miss Prim, like Mr. Thomson, like the telephone operator and her numerous well-paid boyfriends. The other junior staff had formed the Lunch Break Union and had their meals of *mgaiwa* and dried fish prepared for them by one of the laborers in the servants' quarters at the back of the house. The rest contented themselves with boiled or raw cassava and bananas down by the Post Office.

He did not go to lunch. He could not start now. He had trained his stomach not to expect such a luxury. Instead, he drank a glass of water at noon and then went in the usual direction to a definite spot under a tree in the extensive gardens. There he loosened his tie, took off his jacket and shoes, and with obvious relief lay down to sleep, ignoring the inevitable rumblings of his stomach.

The beginning of the afternoon session always found him back at his desk banging away furiously. He could go on like that the whole afternoon, the noises of the keys interrupted at intervals by the loud guffaws of laughter from the secondary school kids.

There were six of them, four boys and two girls. Chingaipe knew intuitively who was going out with whom from the occasional snatches of dialogue he caught while changing carbons or rummaging in his drawers or puzzling over the handwriting of the Higher Clerical Officer. In one of them, he had heard the kid called Mavuto talking to the older girl.

"Of course, there are different types of hair," he had remarked loudly.

"Mine is called love hair," she had replied, unabashed.

"I'm not talking about your wig, baby."

They would have gone on and on like that if one of the others had not noticed how rigidly Chingaipe had sat and so told the two to shut up. Chingaipe had continued to grope about the bottom right-hand drawer, embarrassed. He did not know where the world was going to. In his day … In his day … He found what he was looking for.

True, he did not go to lunch and his wife prepared a meal for him as soon as he reached home after work. Nambewe. Up at half past five to heat the water for her husband. Up at half past five to prepare porridge for their children to eat before going to school. One of them was now at secondary school. Chingaipe hoped he would not turn into a brash, unmannered kid like Mabvuto, in an office like this. He was trying to teach *his* children the meaning of work, determination, perseverance. Nambewe. Up at half past five to get her husband and children ready for the day. Nambewe, washing dirty pots and plates. Cleaning. Pounding grain for flour. Nambewe in her missionary blue *chirundu* and *nyakura*, a load of firewood on her head down the mountain slopes. Nambewe, smiling tenderly at him before they went off to sleep at night. Nambewe …

Chingaipe brought the puncher near the typewriter. He stood up with a sheaf of papers and inserted them in the space ready to punch holes in them. He tensed the muscles of his right hand and pressed down. Crunch. There was only one hole in the papers. The other half of the puncher had broken under the force, and fell on the floor with a loud clink.

The office was very still as Chingaipe groped about the floor for the broken piece. He looked from it back to the puncher. He pulled the sheaf of papers and laid them flat on the table. He sat down again and stared at the single hole.

Nambewe. Up at half past five to …

Chingaipe stood up again. He picked up the puncher and the broken piece and went past the now busy young clerks ostentatiously poring over their files. He opened the door to the passage and knocked on the door marked "Higher Clerical Officer" in large letters. He entered on hearing the growl, "Come in."

He stood in front of the huge desk littered with trays, files, notebooks, ledger cards, and looked at the man behind. The Higher Officer was in his late forties. He had sparse hair—a fact which he attempted to hide by having his hair cut very short each time he went to the barber's. But one cannot hide a fast-receding hairline. The cheap spectacles he wore glinted dully as he looked up slowly.

"Yes?"

"The puncher is broken, sir," Chingaipe said slowly.

"The puncher is broken, sir," mimicked the Higher Clerical Officer. "You mean 'I broke the puncher,' don't you?"

"Yes, sir."

"You junior clerks, copy typists, and messengers," he spat out, "you can't be trusted to do even a simple job without a catastrophe happening. What will happen to this department if equipment is broken every day?"

"I was only trying to punch holes in a few letters I had typed, sir," Chingaipe explained.

"And you decided to break the puncher in the process?" the Higher Clerical Officer enquired. "You will have to see Mr. Thomson about this. We cannot allow this sort of thing to happen every day. I'm tired of all you junior clerks' tricks and inefficiency on the job. I swear some of you will get the sack before month end."

Chingaipe stood quite still as the Higher Clerical Officer's face swam in front of him. Nambewe. Up at half past five to ...

"You must report this personally to Mr. Thomson immediately," the Higher Clerical Officer announced. "I cannot deal with this case myself."

"Yes, sir."

Chingaipe walked mechanically out of the room and down the passage. The puncher heavy in his hand. He went on, knocked, and entered Mr. Thomson's office.

"Good afternoon, Chingaipe."

"Good afternoon, sir," Chingaipe stammered. "The Higher Clerical Officer told me to see you, sir. I was trying to punch holes ..."

"And the puncher broke?"

"Yes, sir."

"Gosh!" Mr. Thomson exclaimed. "You must be strong, Chingaipe."

Chingaipe was silent.

"Tell the Higher Clerical Office to make out a local purchase order for a dozen punchers."

"Yes, sir."

Four o'clock. Time to go home. Chingaipe opened the bottom right-hand drawer. He took out the dust cover, locked the typewriter, and covered it. He stood up to go. The "IN" tray was empty. So was the building as he left. He said a tired goodbye to the night watchman.

"Tidzaonananso mawa, achimwene."

The Spider's Web

He had woven his web round one corner of the room, hanging down from the ceiling. Anyone occupying the cell cot could see the faint shiny outlines of the extensive network he had built for himself. The intersecting rafters made a convenient palace. The spider could retire into this tower and peer down on his domain to watch the movements of prospective victims without fear of being touched—not even by human hands. John Ndatani could see the brown, dried-up corpses curled in unnatural positions to mark the spider's dietary progress. Round these skeletal specimens were the tiny threads that shackled them forever in a suspended tomb that trembled for brief moments in the draught which blew in from the small window high up in the wall at the opposite end of the cell. The tiny forms would be unlucky mosquitoes. Ndatani recognized the familiar shapes of dead flies dotted here and there along the ribs of the fine web.

Come into my parlor, said the spider to the fly ...

That is what the man had said to Ndatani that same morning, although not in exactly those terms. And Ndatani, with a head that was threatening to explode at any moment, had gazed blearily at him as if he could not figure out how on earth the man had come to be standing on the doorstep with Ndatani opening the door for him. The blue car standing twenty yards away sorted out some of the confusion. But comprehension dawns slowly on a brain waking from a dozen double gin and tonics on top of an equal number of beers.

"Will you come with us, sir?" the man had repeated patiently. "We have a few questions to ask you at the office."

Ndatani shivered slightly and continued to gawp at the man.

"You'd better get dressed."

Ndatani looked slowly down at himself and realized that he was in his underwear only. Getting dressed seemed suddenly to be the most urgent task at that moment. He lurched into the bedroom and slumped down, with a groan, on the bed. A pair of trousers lay crumpled on the floor.

His shoes and socks looked as though they had been dropped at random in his erratic progress from the door to the bed the previous night.

"You'd better hurry, sir," the man spoke from the bedroom doorway. "We haven't got the whole morning."

Ndatani remembered his mission. He gripped his head again for few moments before he stood up. He went unsteadily to where his shirt lay under a chair. All the time he seemed to be debating whether to go back to sleep or comply with the order to get dressed. He put his left hand against the wall to steady the dizzy moments of pulling his trousers on. The socks and shoes needed longer. That operation required sitting down again on the bed. Only then did he speak.

"Where are we going?"

"To the office."

"To ... the ... office?" He sat up slowly, as though this information had only just percolated and registered in his befuddled mind.

"Come on," the man ordered again.

Ndatani stood up again and mutely brushed past the man. His zombie-like state continued as he watched the man lock the front door and motion him to the parked car. Someone opened the door from the inside and he got in mechanically. He closed his eyes again as a hundred axes seemed to be at work in his head. So he showed no particular interest in the other occupants of the car. He re-opened his eyes as the car started. The eyes remained fixed on the back of the neck of the man in the front seat. Buildings floated by and disappeared past his indifferent vision as he sank slowly back to sleep.

They had to help him out of the car ...

Ndatani could not help noticing the spider as he came out of his parlor on thin, spindly black legs.

If he decides to spin on one of his webs, he could land on me ...

The spider was directly in line with Ndatani's vision: brooding eyes, almost hypnotic in his stare. He was of an older generation. He looked so ancient. As Ndatani continued to look at him he seemed to take on different shapes advancing and receding. Ndatani gazed fascinated at the coat. The swollen, green, moss-like stomach looked well-fed. The red eyes glittered greedily at the most recent victim, supine below him.

If he decides to spin down on one of his webs, he is surely going to land on me …

The repulsive face of an old man grinning evilly at him crossed Ndatani's vision.

"It's only a spider," Ndatani muttered to himself.

The face grew larger and seemed to have acquired a mane that was smothering Ndatani. Yet he could not take his eyes off the spider to breathe.

If he decides to spin down on one of his webs, he must land on me …

Ndatani wondered if the spider had a family back there in his palace. He concluded that he had not. The thought of a pack of such malignant creatures sent a shudder of revulsion through him. Imagine the spider spinning down one of his webs and landing on him, wrapping his repellent black legs round his throat. Mrs. Spider caressing his cheek with her green, mossy stomach. Young Spider's red eyes peering into his own.

Ndatani jumped out of bed and rushed to the cell door. The bars shook as he yelled at the top of his voice. The empty passageway echoed back hollowly, "Let me out of here!"

***

John Ndatani paused for a moment on the steps of the Club Tropicana. His eyes had caught the fleeting reflection of light on water to the left. He went closer to investigate. It was a shallow pool in which were beautiful goldfish forever trapped in the game of survival of the fittest. They swam gracefully, lazily, and seemed totally unaware of the man-made trap they apparently enjoyed themselves in. A little one was playing hide-and-seek with its mate in the green algae floating near the surface. Ndatani wondered if the black shapes at the bottom of the pool were rocks or crabs.

"Hi, there!"

"Eh?" Ndatani straightened up quickly. The girl facing him was the type to produce explosive monosyllables.

"I said, 'Hi!'" Ndatani let his breath out slowly. He did not want to explain that it was not the manner of delivery but the producer of the familiar greeting that had disoriented him somewhat. The clinging, long, green dress encased vibrant material sending out messages confirmed by the smile.

"Haven't seen you here before, though."

"I shouldn't think so," Ndatani answered.

"You a visitor here?"

"Not exactly." He had regained his composure. "I only came back this afternoon."

"O-oh. A been-to. Super." The telegraphic signs were frantic. "Buy me a drink and tell me all about it."

"Gladly."

Ndatani looked back into the greenish pool to see if the black shapes had moved. They had not. He sighed and followed the girl. The perfume she was wearing floated to his nostrils as they mounted the steps to the entrance.

Come into my parlor, said the spider to the fly ...

There was a vacant table in one corner of the room which they headed for. They sat down and Ndatani surveyed the room. They were in a section of the club where customers could drink and talk without raising their voices. Music could be heard in the next room. As it was, this room was half-filled with a cross-section of the population: half-a-dozen white faces pretending they only stopped for one for the ditch, and scattered browned-off faces of the colored community. The majority were blacks.

"Has it changed?"

"Not much. Although last time I was here, they didn't have that wall separating the dance floor from the room."

"Were you out that long?" She sounded genuinely interested. "That wall was built three years ago."

"I've been out for five years."

"Tell me about it," she invited me again, "over a drink."

"I'm sorry." He waved to a tired-looking waiter at the opposite end of the room. "I was taking in the face-lift."

The waiter, who had previously seemed unoccupied, found something else to do. He busied himself wiping one of the tables near the one where most of the whites were seated.

"That fellow seems to have forgotten he acknowledged my wave."

"Maybe he thought you were only greeting him."

"I don't know him from my prodigal grandfather."

"They're always like that," the girl said. "They provide service to a black man without the smile and without the promptness."

"Really?"

"You'll either have to buttonhole a waiter when you find one, or go to the bar, order, and carry back your own drinks."

"Does the management know about this?"

"Old Gecko couldn't care less."

"Who?"

"The club has changed hands since you left," the girl explained. "The girls call him Old Gecko. He sticks like crazy once he's interested in a girl."

"That makes two of us." He stood up. "I'll see about the drinks. What's your poison, Miss …?"

"Mary. I'll have a gin and tonic."

"Call me John. Won't be long."

Mary watched the tall, lean shape wind its way to the waiter and speak to him. They both looked in her direction as Ndatani gestured to where she was seated. The waiter nodded and went to the bar. Ndatani walked slowly back with a slight frown on his broad forehead. But by the time he had reached the table he was showing a row of strong white teeth.

"I told that fellow what he's supposed to be in this place."

"Only don't hold your breath."

"We'll see." He settled back in his chair dusted the sleeves of his black jacket. He straightened his black tie and leaned forward to her. "I won't ask what a nice chick like you is doing in a dump like this and all that, but I sure am curious."

"I'll give you the old line. Couldn't go to university. Had a man friend in an influential position who promised to give me a job and eventually marry me. He had a family and kids already. Can't go back to the village. I'd be bored stiff. I work here as a free-lance customer bait."

"I thought they didn't allow that sort of thing in this country anymore."

"No." The red lips opened in a mischievous grin. "Normally I don't advertise. But the night is long, and I took a fancy to you."

"I'm flattered." Ndatani paused while the waiter plonked two glasses absent-mindedly down and left with the money, without a smile. He ignored him and went on. "I gather they raided this place once."

"A few times, in fact."

"Were you ever taken in?"

"No. I have a friend who tells me about these things. I went to other pastures."

"Oh."

"Not that the raids solve matters. The girls were later turned loose with strict warnings not to come back."

"And no one took the warnings seriously?"

"They have to earn a living somehow."

This was rather delicate ground and Ndatani decided to change the subject.

"Would you like to dance?"

"Super!" Mary wriggled out of the chair. "I was wondering when you'd stumble on that idea."

Ndatani smiled quietly to himself. This girl needed careful treatment: intelligence went with her beauty. As they finished their drinks, he wondered what the night would be like. He bought tickets at the entrance to the dance floor and they both went in.

A five-man group was giving the customers their money's worth. The crowd was a macrocosm of the lounge. The only difference was that there was more action and noise here. Couples clung desperately to each other with the intensity of unfulfilled passions. The band whipped them to a state of abandonment of fear, worry, and reality. Here the illusion of complete freedom could be seen through the subdued lights, the smoke, the clink of glasses, loud voices, and the cacophonous music. Mary's colleagues seemed to be fully engaged too. It was obvious who would go to bed with whose.

A Reggae number assaulted the ear-drums:

> *You better come into my parlor,*
> *Said the spider to the fly* ...

After the first two numbers, the night took a definite pattern. Dance, drink, talk ... Dance, drink, talk. Tongues loosened and a running off at the mouth set in. Ndatani's suspicions that he was drunk were confirmed several times when he heard himself loudly sharing his secret hopes and ambitions with Mary and anyone else who cared to listen. The girl grew more and more interested and interesting as she enveloped him more intimately in her generous bosom. Ndatani was past caring. Five years away from home is a long time. Immediate immersion into the rhythm of native life was more important. And what better rhythmizer than Mary?

In the flow of life as he allowed nature to take its course, Ndatani was dimly aware of slumping over Mary's shoulder. Ages later, her voice floated out to him enquiring if he was all right, and after a millennium, a call for a taxi. Hands supported him to a car. He crumpled into a seat. A void ... Faint recollections of creaking bed springs, sweaty bodies, and another blank ...

The banging of the door seemed to detonate something in his skull. He held his head in both hands and tried to stop it from shattering at the seams. His exploring hand met sheets and blankets. Maybe she had gone to answer the door. The banging persisted under his skull. Ndatani mouthed an unintelligible curse.

"Answer the blasted door, Mary!" he shouted.

There was no answer except the continued banging on the door. He got to his feet groggily and gazed blankly about him. This was not the room he had proposed to spend the night in. And what had happened to Mary?

"Mary!" he shouted. "Ouw, my head. Mary!"

Another Writer ~~Taken~~

1

It was a few minutes before noon, and I was packing my briefcase slowly, when Zinenani, an old friend now working in the capital city, burst in.

"Alekeni!" he shouted unceremoniously.

"Hi!"

"When did you get back?"

"Get back?"

"I thought you'd gone abroad?"

"It won't be for a month or so."

"But the whole capital is full of rumors of your having gone already, and decided to stay on."

"Stay on?"

"Defected is the word."

"Defected? Why?"

"Because of what happened to Ndasauka."

"But I wasn't involved in that."

"Rumor has it that since your fellow writer was detained you decided to skip the country."

"But why should I do that? I haven't done anything that would make me go into exile."

"Believe me, when I saw you walk up to your office a few minutes ago, I thought I was seeing a ghost. The rumors were that strong. I came up just to make sure I was seeing right."

"But I was on the radio two days ago."

"That could have been pre-recorded."

"That's true. Anyway, you can tell my well-wishers in the capital that I'm still around."

"But you'll still be going abroad?"

"I can't miss that opportunity."

"The rumors aren't anticipating your exile?"

"Believe me, if I had wanted to go into exile, I would have done so years ago when I was away studying in the UK and USA. The thought had seriously occurred to me then, but after toying with it, I realized I'm deep down an ancestral worshipper. I also discovered that I cannot write the genuine stuff when I'm on foreign soil. I decided to brave my own country, and here I still am."

"It's good the rumors were just that. We need fellows like you around."

"What are you doing here, for that matter?"

"Consultations."

The phone rang. I let it ring.

"It's nice to see you, all the same."

"I've got to be going." Zinenani turned to the door.

"See you again," I waved him off and lifted the receiver.

"Hello?"

"This is Chodziwa-dziwa."

It was my kid brother. He had not been in touch for a long time. He too worked in the capital.

"How are you?"

"Fine. I'm actually speaking from your house."

"When did you come down?"

"I just arrived. I wanted to talk to you."

"I'll be right over. It's lunch time, anyhow."

As I finished packing my briefcase, I puzzled over what Zinenani had said. The rumor was getting slightly stale. Just yesterday, I had been waylaid by a colleague's wife in the supermarket.

"Alekeni, come here!"

She took me by the hand and literally dragged me between two food counters. She was so enthusiastic, I got worried someone might suspect we were going to embrace each other or something, the way she furtively looked around and then drew near me as if she wanted to feel me.

"So," she heaved a sign of relief, "you're not gone!"

"Gone where?"

"Taken by the police."

"Why should the police take me?"

"Because of Ndasauka."

"But I don't even know what he's inside for."

"You don't need to know to be implicated."

"I know, but in this case it's just too far-fetched."

"You're a friend of his, and a writer, too."

"Even then."

It had ended like that, leaving me thoroughly peeved at the source of the rumor. Rumor in Mtalika diffused at the speed of sound: word of mouth, telephone, letter, even telepathy. It was said that even before you decided to seduce your friend's wife, people would know about it already and actively make sure it came about. Before long, I would end up believing in the rumor myself, even when right now I was still in Mtalika, getting into my own car to drive from my office home to have lunch with my family and kid brother. A free man.

"Daddy! Daddy!"

My five-year-old always ran up to the garage doors to meet me as soon as he heard the car in the driveway. Between our dog and him, I could not tell who gave me the warmer welcome. Sometimes they almost tripped over each other in the rush to meet me with cries and barks. It was all overwhelming.

"Your brother is here," were my wife's welcoming words.

"I know."

"He's in the sitting room."

I walked through the dining room to the lounge, to find Chodziwadziwa flipping through a popular magazine. He looked up and grinned sheepishly. Something was bothering him.

"So it's not true," was his greeting as I joined him, sitting down.

"What?"

"That you are missing."

"Missing?" This was getting to be too enormous to be funny.

"A man came round to my place two days ago to say that something had happened involving a friend of yours, that your friend had been taken, and that you had disappeared without trace."

"This is ridiculous. Who was this man?"

"I don't know, and he refused to identify himself. He said he just wanted your relatives to know that you could not be found."

It was wearisome, if not monstrous. I reviewed my involvement with

Ndasauka again.

2

I knew I was going too fast, but could do nothing about it. I knew I was too agitated to be driving at that speed, yet I still maintained it, even when I kept going off the road at each small bend. I knew I had taken one too many, but it was too late to start regretting it. I knew I could not talk about Ndasauka rationally with his best friend by my side.

"Surely," I detected the hoarseness in my voice, "you must know something he was involved in?"

"I'm telling you I don't."

"You don't know, or you don't want to discuss it?"

"I don't know anything that he was doing for the police to be interested in him.

"You're his closest friend."

"That doesn't mean he told me his entire life history."

"You were there when the police came to get him."

"It's very simple. I had invited him out to lunch at the club for a change. We had just finished the meal and were having a drink before going back to work, when they found us at the bar."

"They knew you were in there?"

"That's where they found us. I didn't know what was happening at first. One of them came over and called Ndasauka out. After a few minutes, another one came in, looking for nothing in particular. When Ndasauka didn't come back after fifteen minutes, I went out to investigate. I found him in handcuffs."

"You mean they handcuffed him right outside the club?"

"It created quite a sensation. There was a small crowd when I went out. I followed the police van to the office. There was another crowd as they took him up to his office."

"Still in handcuffs?"

"Yes. Another contingent was already in the office going through his papers. I learnt this from the secretary."

"How did she take it?"

"Scared. So grey she looked almost white. She couldn't type, read, crochet, or phone. I understand they threatened to arrest her too, if she so much as moved from her chair."

"What were they looking for?"

"Search me."

"It comes back to what you know about all this. If you don't know, and his colleagues don't either, who is there to tell us what is happening?"

"The police."

I nearly exploded, the car swerved, and I hastily righted it again.

I felt cheated out of something in life, and frustrated by the tantalizing thought that perhaps, beneath it all, there was really nothing at all to find. Perhaps the police did not even know what they were looking for. Maybe they only had Ndasauka on suspicion, pending further investigations. If that were the case, Ndasauka would be in for a long, long time. He might not even come out.

The normal detention orders operated for twenty-eight days without formal charges. After that period, formal charges had to be filed, a statement issued, or the detainee released. The Republic of Mandania, however, operated neither with normal detention procedures nor with formal charges. A decade or so before, the country had gone through a spate of detentions of several highly placed persons in the civil service, the armed forces, and the university. All were supposedly suspected of planning a coup. Although five years later most of the detainees had been released, some members from that group were still rotting in the numerous camps dotted around the country.

"Are we going back to the seventies?" was the question everyone asked as soon as Ndasauka was taken, and it was rumored, but never verified, that other members of the citizenry had also been or were about to be detained.

"When the police behave like that, it means they have reached the final act," said someone who had lived through the terrors of the seventies, meaning that the swoop was too dramatic and public to be followed by others of a similar nature.

In the seventies, enough terror had been generated for you to distrust even your relative or neighbor, for fear they might turn out to be one of the numerous informers in the pay of the police. People had disappeared into detention, demise, or exile. The whole period was shrouded in such a terrifying cloak of mystery the media never covered it, no one talked about it in public, social places were emptied, because it was safer to retire to your home after work. However, even within the safety of your home, you feared your servants, even your wife and children, and dreaded a knock at the door, lest it should be your turn to be taken.

3

"Don't get involved in this."

It was the parish priest. He had gone to visit Ndasauka's family and then dropped in to see me.

"How can I get involved in something I don't know anything about?"

I was exasperated. Why was everyone implicating me in the whole thing? The first hint that people thought I would be the next one to go was the surprised faces I met at work the day after Ndsauka was taken.

"When did they let you out?" the secretary had asked me.

"Who? What?"

"People said you had also been taken yesterday. Someone saw the flashing lights of a police van in your drive at seven o'clock last night."

"It's a long drive, and the driver might have been reversing."

"But what was it doing there of all places, and at that time?"

I could never figure out the answer to that one. Nor to the next, which I got from a colleague at coffee time the same day.

"Someone told me you were taken for at least a few hours, if not the whole of last night."

"Who's spreading all these rumors?" I exploded. "I was at home and in bed the whole of last night. Why don't people ask me or my wife or my children, before jumping to conclusions based on non-evidence? I know I went to Ndasauka's office, after I'd heard what had happened to him. I saw the police there. I know I went to his house when I didn't find him at the office. I found the police and Ndasauka there. I was there to see him finally bundled into the police Landrover to be heard of no more. But that was all I did."

It had not been all I did, though. I'd arrived at Ndasauka's home just as he was writing post-dated checks to give to his children—his wife was away in the capital on a six-month course. I paced up and down outside, not knowing whether or not I could go in to speak to him, or, in fact, what I would say to him if I could.

The police crowded him out of the house.

"You must take me too!" Ndasauka's seventy-year-old mother cried as she tottered on crutches to follow the band outside. It was the only clear sign of emotion that was expressed by any member of the family. I do not think the children fully understood what was happening, the oldest being only thirteen.

"Don't worry, mother, he'll come back soon," one of the plain clothes men said unconvincingly as they went over to the covered Landrover parked just beyond the garage. Another police saloon was next to it. So many cars and officers for just one man.

"Excuse me," I introduced myself, "I'm a friend of Ndasauka's and I would like to know what's happening."

"Orders from the government: We are to take him to the capital."

"Where in the capital?" It was automatic.

"We can't say."

"But I do have to tell his wife where he's being taken."

"You can't do that. You must not discuss with anyone what has happened today, until you hear from us."

"When will that be?"

"Tomorrow morning."

"But these kids will be alone all night with their old grandmother if his wife is not informed immediately. Who's going to look after them tonight?"

"I'm sorry, those are our instructions."

"Can I talk to Ndasauka?"

"Of course."

I went over to him.

"Look," I whispered, although it was not necessary since the police could also hear me. "Do you know what this is all about?"

"All I know," he said loudly, "Is that I'm being taken to the capital on government orders."

"What would you like me to do?"

He looked at the cluster of mute kids a few feet away. I thought someone would burst into tears. He cleared his throat.

"Look after the kids." He straightened up.

I watched him walk to the police car, flanked by the Special Branch men. They climbed in the back door of the Landrover, sitting him in the middle. The driver shut the doors, went round to the front, opened his door, got in, and shut it too. He turned on the ignition, engaged the gears, and drove off. The saloon followed. No sirens. No tears. That was the last we saw of him.

"Pirira is arriving by the trailer tonight." The parish priest brought me back to the present.

"She knows?"

"Of course. Could you pick her up? I have a meeting with the bishop, and it threatens to be a long one."

"That's all right. I'll meet her."

And so began the longest night in my life. The "trailer," as the late night bus was called, was aptly nicknamed. It took the whole night to reach Mtalika from the capital, when other buses took no more than three hours. I had not known these details before, and had gone to the bus station at nine o'clock, to check on Ndasauka's wife. They told me it would arrive at eleven. At eleven it still did not appear. Nor at one.

I parked by one of the shops with lighted fronts near the bus station and tried to sleep in the car. At three, another car came and parked behind mine. I raised a sleepy head. The other man recognized me.

"You're not waiting for the trailer, are you?"

"Yes."

"You're too early. It won't be here till four-thirty or later."

"But why didn't they tell me that before, so I could sleep at home first?"

"They didn't know, either. It's quite erratic."

"Surely they could have phoned?"

"Once it has left the capital, it stops at every single imaginable place to drop or pick up any mail or passengers at every single trading center. It's useless keeping track of it. Those who know about its unpredictability wait until dawn before venturing to meet it."

I looked at my watch: three-fifteen. If I went home, I would probably sleep until midday. I decided to stay where I was.

The trailer groaned to a halt at four-thirty, dragging the mail van, from whence its nickname. I walked across.

"Pirira," I greeted Mrs Ndasauka. It was painful to try to smile.

"What happened?" she sobbed. She looked as if she had been crying all the way and was on the verge of collapse.

"The car is over there."

I got her bag and walked briskly away. She had to trot after me.

"It's like this," I said as I drove off. "We really don't know what's happening."

It was no consolation. I let her get what was left out of her system and drove in silence all the way to her house.

"Mummy!" was the delighted cry of the youngest boy, as he rushed out to my car. The joy of seeing his mother and the reason for her being there were too irreconcilable.

"I'll be in touch." I drove off.

"I'm sorry to get you involved like this," the parish priest had continued. "You're a fellow writer and a friend of his. You should check your travel documents."

"How can I get involved when I don't know what the hell it is all about?" I was angry again.

4

I turned into the side road leading up to the police camp, and stopped at the barrier just inside the iron gates. There was a flurry of activity in the little hut on the side of the road. Two armed men emerged. One marched purposefully toward the car.

"Name and address?"

He leaned through the open window, surveyed me and the interior of the car. He paused by my left hand, which was still holding the gear stick. I ignored the bayonet waving half-a-foot away from my throat and supplied the information.

"Can we help you?"

I mentioned my desire to visit one of the top-ranking officers.

"Just a moment, sir." He marched back to the hut. I could see him phoning.

I was wondering why the police had to be so armed. There were road blocks manned by heavily armed police at several points on either side of Mtalika town. It seemed as if Mandania was in a perpetual state of siege or under curfew. As far as I knew, the nearest war was across the border, and it had nothing to do with Mandania.

"Just obeying orders, sir." The man came back. "I have to ask his permission to let you through."

I shrugged my shoulders and asked for directions. The barrier was lifted, I drove past slowly, and waved back at the mock salute I was given by the other man.

"Alekeni! Long time no see."

The officer, in civilian clothes, pumped my hand with exaggerated enthusiasm as I got out of the car.

"We just wave at each other as we drive past in town."

"This is indeed a pleasure. Come in."

I didn't know if my mission could be discussed in the house with half-a-dozen kids milling around.

"Thank you!" I said all the same, and followed him inside.

The sitting room was filled with enough furniture for two houses. He waved me to a sumptuous seat, into which I sank up to my waist. I bobbed up again, and sat forward on the shallower edge of the chair.

"This is Alekeni, my old school-mate," he introduced me to a parade of sons and daughters who detached themselves from various corners and rooms and advanced an arm and a shy smile to me. They filed back to their occupations afterward, like a small regiment.

Brief pause.

I decided to plunge straight into the purpose of my visit. He jerked forward.

"Yes," he spoke rapidly, "Ndasauka. I heard about it. Routine, of course. I'm kept informed of what is happening."

"The problem is," I continued, "that WE don't know what is happening, and we are really worried about it. It's now a week and there's no news about his whereabouts, nor even the reasons for his being taken."

"But why come to me?" He was very agitated. "It's not really my department. I'm only kept informed as a matter of course."

"For the simple reason that we were at school together, we got to be friends, even though we haven't kept it up since. Also, his wife said you go to the same church. She, in fact, is the one who suggested I should come to see you directly."

"You realize this is a delicate matter?"

"But we don't know anything."

"I'm telling you it's a delicate matter. If anyone knew you came to see me about it, I would be in trouble."

"Surely you can mention at least to his wife the nature of the suspicions or speculations as to why he was taken?"

"It's too sensitive."

"I take it it's not a criminal charge, then."

"In his case, it wouldn't be that."

"It's political, then?"

"Look, I only got to know about it as a matter of routine. I didn't enquire further into the details, although I saw his name on the list."

"There are others involved, too?"

"Yes, and I trust you appreciate the fact that I can't just lift the phone and call the Special Branch to tell me the details?"

"I do, but surely on the list there was some explanation why the people had to be taken?"

"That's why I'm saying it's too delicate to discuss with you at the moment. Give me a few days and perhaps I can let you know what can be safely told to you."

"When can I get in touch with you again?"

"I'll get in touch with you."

When we parted, I had a strong suspicion he would not contact me again, and that I had lost an old school friend forever. I wondered as I drove out past the armed guards again if the country hadn't been in a state of emergency all along and I hadn't known it. It was too delicate to announce publicly, and so too would the next one to be taken.

MGP505: 10/6/64-25/6/71

200/3104/M/64

Mkwinda Village,
T.A. Chigaru,
P.O. Kasiya,
Mandania.
22 May, 1964

Mines Superintendent,
Golpha Mines,
Witwatersrand,
Johannesburg,
South Africa.

Dear Sir,

Mr. John Matekenya

I am writing on behalf of Mrs. Otilya Matekenya who wants urgently to get in touch with her husband, Mr. John Matekenya, of Mkwinda Village, T.A. Chigaru, P.O. Kasiya, Mandania. he left the country on 20 January, 1959. He was last heard of under your employ.

We would be grateful if you could help us trace him.

Yours sincerely,

Paulo Lupiya

Paulo Lupiya
for: Mrs. O. Matekenya

200/3104/M/64/2

Golpha Mines,
Witwatersrand,
Johannesburg,
South Africa.
12 June, 1964

Mrs. O. Matekenya,
Mkwinda Village,
T.A. Chigaru,
P.O. Kasiya,
Mandania.

Dear Madam,

Mr. John Matekenya

    With reference to your letter dated 22 May, 1964, requesting information as to the whereabouts of the above, we would like to inform you that he left Golpha Mines on 10 June 1964, on Wenela flight SA068, dep. Jan Smuts Airport 08:10, arr. Mtalika Airport 10:45.

    Yours sincerely,

Mathews Thuku

Mathews Thuku

for: Mines Superintendent

mt/PT

G.P. 16B

T.1

TELEGRAM

MANDANIA

Ministry of Transport and Communications

A.   DEPARTMENT OF POSTS AND TELECOMMUNICATIONS

No. **26/17/6/64/KAS**

Class	Date Stamp	Words	Date	Time Handed in
		21	17/6/64	14:05

Route and Service Instructions

--

SENT

TO: PLEASE WRITE DISTINCTLY

CIVIL AVIATION, MTALIKA AIRPORT

BOX 12, MTALIKA

Charge
K   t

At. **Kasiya**

To. **Mtalika**

By. **SMT**

WANTED INFORMATION JOHN MATEKENYA ARRIVED WENELA FLIGHT SA 068 TENTH JUNE

FROM: **MRS. MATEKENYA**   NOT TO BE TELEGRAPHED

Signature of Sender ....   Address   **Poste Restante, Kasiya**

N.B.—The Government is not liable for losses incurred through incorrect transmission, delay or non-delivery of Telegrams. In the case of Reply Paid Messages, the sender's address should also appear in the "FROM".

CA/PF/001/64

Civil Aviation,
Mtalika Airport,
P.O. Box 12,
Mtalika.
18 June, 1964

Mrs. O. Matekenya,
Poste Restante,
Kasiya.

Dear Madam,

Mr. John Matekenya

All Wenela passengers board a Special Hire Bus from the airport to Mtalika Bus Station. We would advise you to enquire from the Station Master, Mtalika as to the above person's whereabouts.

Yours sincerely,

Fides Taibu

Fides Taibu

for: The Director of Civil Aviation

ft/SM

G.P. 16B

T.1

TELEGRAM

MANDANIA

Ministry of Transport and Communications

A. **DEPARTMENT OF POSTS AND TELECOMMUNICATIONS**

No. **29/20/6/64/KAS**

Class	Date Stamp	Words	Date	Time Handed in	
		19	20/6/64	11:05	SENT
			Route and Service Instructions	---	
			Charge K t		At. **Kasiya** To. **Mtalika** By. **PP**

TO: PLEASE WRITE DISTINCTLY

STATION MASTER, BUS STATION

BOX 216, MTALIKA

WANTED INFORMATION JOHN MATEKENYA SPECIAL HIRE

MTALIKA AIRPORT TO MTALIKA TENTH JUNE

FROM: **MRS. MATEKENYA** NOT TO BE TELEGRAPHED

Signature of Sender .... Address **Poste Restante, Kasiya** ....

The Bus Station,
P.O. Box 216,
Mtalika.
21 June 1964

Mrs. Matekenya,
Poste Restante,
Kasiya.

Dear Madam,

Mr. John Matekenya

We regret to inform you that we have no information on the above-named. It would be too great a demand on the company's resources to keep track of every single passenger who used its public transport facilities.

Yours sincerely

Peter Chigonegone

Peter Chigonegone
Station master

> *I am back on home soil. The land of milk and honey. How good it is to breathe the sweet air of Mandania again. Goodbye to the fumes of the mines. I will never go back. Five years is a long time away from my loved ones. I wonder how my wife is. And little Sipoko. He must be a big boy now. The mchona is back with lots and lots of money and presents. Mkwinda Village, here I come. I think I shall take a taxi and surprise those villagers.*

10/6/64
From: <u>Mtalika</u>   to: <u>Kasupe</u>
Fare: <u>£15 (fifteen pounds)</u>
Comments:
The passenger had agreed to pay the above sum, but on nearing Kasupe he started complaining that the charge was too high. He cursed me in Chilapalapa and threatened to fix me. He said he was not going to pay me. He would show me what people do in Jo'burg. I was afraid to drive him to Mkwinda Village because I knew he was not going to pay, so I drove straight to the Police Station. He did not say anything to the Police Officer so he was put in a cell. I am waiting for the Police to contact me again on the matter.

Mine boy returns home—to jail

John Matekenya appeared in court today for refusing to pay his taxi fare from Mtalika to Kasupe. Matekenya returned home straight to jail yesterday after working in Johannesburg mines for five years. He claimed he had paid the fare. The magistrate commented on the flimsy evidence to support his story. Matekenya was sentenced to twelve months.

The taxi driver involved in this case, Mr. Lysense Kadzioche, has been working for Ahmed Taxi Services for ten years. Ahmed Taxi Services have got branches in Mtalika and Kasupe. Asked to comment on the case, Mr. Kadzioche shook his head. "Strange case," he muttered. "In all my years in the taxi business I've never met anything like it."

Of Life, Love, and Death

G.P. 16B   T.1

TELEGRAM

MANDANIA

Ministry of Transport and Communications

A.   DEPARTMENT OF POSTS AND TELECOMMUNICATIONS

No. **5/22/6/64/KAS**

SENT

Class	Date Stamp	Words	Date	Time Handed in
		16	22/6/64	07:42

Route and Service Instructions

—

Charge

K   t

At **Kasiya**
To **Mtalika**
By **PP**

TO: PLEASE WRITE DISTINCTLY
        COURT CLERK, URBAN COURT
        BOX 114, KASUPE

PLEASE INFORM NAME OF PRISON JOHN MATEKENYA

FROM: **MRS. MATEKENYA**   NOT TO BE TELEGRAPHED

Signature of Sender ....   Address __**Poste Restante, Kasiya**__

N.B.—The Government is not liable for losses incurred through incorrect transmission, delay or non-delivery of Telegrams.
In the case of Reply Paid Messages, the sender's address should also appear in the "FROM".

104

Otilya came to see me today. I cannot describe the feelings I had seeing her again after five long years. The Prison Warder did not let her inside. How cruel! We spoke through the bars. How I longed to embrace her! My heart bleeds. Have I come home to these bare walls? The clang of prison doors? Boots on cement and pick axe on rock? I cannot bear twelve months of this.

I had nothing to give my dear Otilya - the police confiscated most of my belongings, gifts, money, and my freedom.

I told Otilya what had happened: I had paid the taxi-man the full amount, but he did not give me a receipt. How can I prove my innocence? Anyway, Otilya is appealing for a review of the case in the High Court. I shall be out soon.

Sipoko did not come. He is coming next time. My son!

8/6/65
M.G.P. 505: 10/6/64 - 10/6/65 Block C is charged with assault and battery of Mr. Lysense Kadzioche of Ahmed Taxi Services. The warder on duty reported that he heard shouts for help in the cell where the prisoner was kept. He rushed in and found the prisoner strangling the visitor. Mr. Kadzioche insists on laying a charge against the prisoner.

M.G.P. 505: 10/6/64 - 10/6/65, who was due for release in two days time, remains in his cell until the court hearing.

Signed: *P. Thompson*

Peter Thompson
Superintendent for Prisons

> Your Worship, I had only wanted to say hello to John Matekenya and tell him that my taxi was at his service if he wanted it when he was released. He yelled and leapt at me. Suddenly his hands were round my throat. I shouted for help. If the warder hadn't come, I would have been killed. And all because I was trying to be friendly. That fellow is mad ...

15/6/65

M.G.P. 505: 10/6/64 - 10/6/65 is readmitted to this prison for a further term of one year: 15/6/65 - 15/6/66.

Signed: *P. Thompson*
            Peter Thompson
            Superintendent for Prisons

> *Otilya came to see me today. Oh, her accusing eyes ... how could I do it? How could I explain to her? Twelve months in prison for nothing and seeing my tormenter there in front of me, free, and jeering at me - How could I restrain myself?*
>
> *Forgive me, Otilya. Forgive me, Sipoko. I shall be with you soon.*
>
> *God, why are they keeping me here?*

13/6/66
M.G.P. 505: 10/6/64 - 15/6/66 is a curious case. He was due for release (again) in two days time. Mr. Lysense Kadzioche of Ahmed Taxi Services has laid another charge of battery and assault with a dangerous weapon against the prisoner. Mr. Kadzioche was permitted to visit the prisoner. The same thing happened as last year: the prisoner assaulted Kadzioche, this time with a knife. Investigations are under way as to where he obtained this weapon. M.G.P. 505: 10/6/64 - 15/6/66 is in solitary confinement until the court hearing.

Signed: *P. Thompson*
             Peter Thompson
             Superintendent for Prisons

I did not do it! I swear to God above to strike me dead if I touched him. He came in grinning at me. I stared horrified at my tormenter and moved away from him. It was he who rushed at me and beat me. When he saw that I did not do anything he proceeded to hit his head against the wall and shout for help. I knew what would befall me again and I was sick with fear. He produced a knife. I tried to take it away from him and the warder found us struggling on the floor for that knife.

What is to become of me? Am I ever going to see my wife, my son, my relatives at home?

What did I do to him?

> John Matekenya   v.   Lysense Kadzioche
> (1966 / ALR Man. 124)
> High Court of Mandania
> A charge of assault with a dangerous weapon was brought against the defendant, John Matekenya …
>
> John Matekenya   v.   Republic
> (1966 / ALR Man. 125)
> High Court of Mandania
> A charge of disorderly conduct while serving sentence was brought against the defendant …

25/6/66

M.G.P. 505: 10/6/64 - 15/6/66 is back in prison. The term is now five years with hard labour. He is a strange case. Under normal circumstances he would strike one as a mild-mannered man. Apart from the incidents with the taxi driver, Lysense Kadzioche, he has never been a discipline problem. But one never know with these people. He has been to the mines, too.

His wife came to visit him today. She nearly assaulted the warder. Four strong men were needed to remove her from her husband's cell door. I have never seen such a hysterical woman.

Signed: *P. Thompson*
Peter Thompson
Superintendent for Prisons

20/6/71
The warder wouldn't let me see John Matekenya. I told
him I was an old friend of the prisoner and wanted to offer
my taxi to take him home when he was released in a few
days time. He didn't believe me. He told me that each time
I came on a good will visit, it earned the prisoner an
extension. It seems Matekenya has been behaving so well
that the officials would really like to see him out of the
prison without any well-wishers ... we'll see ...

I'll be out in two days time. Yet I fear him. My tormentor will come to visit me again. Maybe today, or tomorrow, or the day they let me out. He will definitely come. I know it! What shall I do? If I kill him, they will hang me. If I don't, he will do something that will make me rot forever. My God, my God! What shall I do?

25/6/71
M.G.P. 505: 10/6/64 - 25/6/71
A full-scale investigation is being undertaken into the
events which led to the suicide by hanging of M.G.P. 505:
10/6/64 - 25/671, John Matekenya. The relatives have
been notified.

Signed: *P. Thompson*
             Peter Thompson
             Superintendent for Prisons

A Visit to Chikanga

I haven't come to you as a patient. I'm a sociologist on a field trip. I know you only treat patients, or help those who come to consult you about their sick relatives. But Chikanga is a famous medicine man, not only in the country but also across the border in Mozambique, Tanzania, Zambia, and Zimbabwe. Even in South Africa. Carloads, busloads, truckloads of people come to take your potions. You tour from village to village and from township to township, administering your medicines or *mchape*, dispensing charms here and herbs there; getting rid of pestilence here and witchcraft there; loosening the rains where they have been tied up by the witches. ...

Yes, yes, I know academics don't believe in witchcraft, magic, or traditional medicines. These are the depressing results of the old colonialists and missionaries. They branded you charlatans, and your practice fell into disrepute. I know how you feel when you see people like me in western dress, wearing western minds, and breathing western arrogance. Yet yours is really a very noble and ancient profession. It has kept the Africans from becoming extinct with pestilences, catastrophes, droughts, and famine. But that's precisely why I have come to you: to write the truth about you for the academics or sceptics, so they can understand what you do in your profession. I hope you don't take these remarks as ingratiating, as a way of getting you to grant me an audience. Far be it from my intentions. I'm on this final year project, you see.

No, no. I'm not just after passing my BSoc degree. As your *nsupa* has divined, my project on traditional healers is only a partial requirement. But I have a personal commitment, too. You know the craze these days, even in academia: back to traditional customs, ancestral wisdom, back to the roots, and all that. Attitudes to indigenous African values and the past have changed. Even the townspeople are now buying traditional insurance policy packages like a *chithumwa* round the waist, incisions on intimate parts of the body, protective charms around the house, in the car and office. This is as it should be. It is part of our traditional culture. Do you know what? I am even a member of the national traditional healers' association. In fact my friends think I also dabble in the dark arts, as they call them, the way I go on about the subject.

This equipment? The camera, tape recorder, note pads, and all that? Oh, don't worry about them. They are just to record our little chat to convince my supervisors that I really had a direct interview with you. Don't be puzzled. In fact, you can find affinities between all this paraphernalia and your bric-à-brac. I am using western technology, scientific methods of analysis and computation, to satisfy western scholarship. They call this technology and yours mumbo-jumbo. It's one of the attitudes I want to correct. I'd rather call yours appropriate technology, that's the buzz expression. I get all hot when the skeptics don't see the obvious parallels between what you do and what modern physicians do. ...

Yes, I know, you would have welcomed me more readily if I had come as a patient. For example, the craze on campus is for higher grades, but you see, I already get high grades in my courses. You could have divined that, couldn't you? And at the moment, I'm in peak condition. I couldn't have feigned even a headache. You would have seen through it, too, so I decided to be honest with you. ...

You're getting old. Traditional healers go to their graves with the vast wisdom they have acquired in life. They don't pass it on to their children and grandchildren. ...

I agree, you have these assistants, nephews and nieces, who are your apprentices. But, again, they have the same tendencies: they don't write articles or books about what they do, the way we do in the university. You don't share your knowledge with outsiders. ...

You say sharing knowledge dilutes it? In our academic world, shared knowledge advances mankind. I know mankind hasn't improved a lot since it emerged from the caves. Look at nuclear weapons, no worse than bows and arrows; look at AIDS, incurable; look at poverty and ignorance; but we are, I mean mankind, is trying, and you could help tremendously by ...

I know, you have helped hundreds and hundreds already and will help hundreds more before you pass away but ...

Help me? But, as I said, I don't need ...

Bewitched? Me? Do I look it? I'm a normal, healthy, intelligent young man. The only diseases I have suffered from and long been cured of are malaria, bilharzia, measles, a headache or two before exams, one or two STDs before AIDS came in, but these are …

A witch's pot in my tummy? How did it get there? My grandmother, Mfitizalimba? How did you know her name? Yes, I was, am still her favorite. Each vacation I go to the village to visit her. …

Me, on witches' rides with her? I'll be doing it even after she's gone? Come on! How come I don't even know I'm on an owl's or hyena's back going to the next graveyard? Even fly to South Africa, you say? Let me tell you something, I have never been out of this country in my life. …

Yes, but what your assistant is showing me is just a tattered, old, open basket. How can anyone ride this *chipapa* to Jo'burg, as you say? *Ninety* people in this thing the size of a dinner plate? You need advanced theory and practice of aerodynamics to fly, my friend, yet all this thing has are some cloth *chithumwa* tied round the edge. …

I know, I talked about affinities or parallels with modern science. But again, as I said, you people work in the dark. Look at you, all I can hear in this gloom is your voice from the inner room. I can't see you. I can't tell whether you're young or old. You must be old, since you were there before I was born. People say there has always been a Chikanga, so we don't know whether you are the original, the son, grandson, or an incarnation. These are the kinds of things I came to ask you about. Come out of the darkness. …

I'm blind, you say, and need to be shown daylight? But I made my way here past your *nsupa*, horns, animal skins, roots, herbs, leaves scattered around your compound. Your assistants kept away the owls and *nzulule* from landing on me. It's only when I entered your consultation room that it became dark. All right, if you can conjure her up in your diviner's mirror, but Mfitizalimba is not a video actress, I warn you. …

Chauta be praised! There she is! I know that *chipini* on the left nostril, protruding lips ready to elongate, swollen stomach—she's the one who must have a pot in her tummy; shrunken dugs, an unwashed *biriwita* tied round her wispy waist. She's almost ageless, that's the way I've known her since my childhood. ...

Your arch-enemy, you say, and that makes me your enemy, too? How could that be? I said I have a major paper to write in sociology. An excuse? Sent by Mfitizalimba? What has grandmother got to do with the requirements of a BSoc degree? Mfitizalimba's agent on her final mission of revenge? She wanted to combine her potent charms with my brains? Without infiltrating your stronghold she couldn't do much? ...

Look here, it took me more than twelve years of primary and secondary education to reach the university. I'm in my fourth and final year now. How could I ...?

Witchcraft works in mysterious ways? It's like industrial espionage? Mfitizalimba was training me and now wants me to learn all your secrets to destroy you? Why? You had exposed her as a witch for tying up the rains in one of the worst droughts in the country, and she has never forgiven you for it? ...

How come she can still fight you if you gave her *mwabvi?* I thought after you neutralize their powers, they can't go back to witchery, on pain of death? You were young then and had left out some ingredients? Since then she has been plotting how to exact her own revenge against you? ...

But you can't take it out on me: you, yourself, said I was blind. I'm innocent. I didn't know I had a witch's pot in my tummy. I don't know I fly and dance in the graveyards every night. How can you use me? ...

She'll know you did it to me? She'll be so mad she'll come after you and you'll be ready for her? ...

You won't get away with it! Everyone knows I'm here: my professor, the college administration. I had to get permission to be off campus. I even wrote to my parents about this visit. They'll go to the police. ...

No need to kill me? Disappear? No? Turn into a *ndondocha?* No? Yes, yes, I've seen some of my friends go mad before completing their programs. In fact, one of my friends is at the asylum. He's beyond repair. I'll go the same way? But I'm innocent, I tell you. Mfitizalimba ...?

She only taught me stories, songs, and the folk wisdom she had accumulated down the years. These are the ones I have used in some of my papers to get high grades, because they were original. I've even published in international journals, just imagine, even before I graduate! ...

I'm also graduating to be a great wizard conjointly with my BSoc? Mfitizalimba was going to give me the final initiation rites in witchdom at graduation? I'm the most dangerous wizard in the country, educated in both worlds? So I've got to be eliminated before graduation? ...

Look, Mr Chikanga, you're a man of many rains. Let's try to be rational about this. To be a witch or wizard, you have got to be a consenting adult. In my childhood, you say? But I have also got to be a conscious being, I mean, at least know that I'm a practicing sorcerer. Hundreds and hundreds are sorcerers without their knowledge or consent? But that's criminal! Who does this to them? ...

No criminality or rationalization in witchdom? All values reversed: human flesh is for eating, the best source is relatives, flying in baskets without engines? ...

But I'm not a witch, I tell you! I'm a sociology student working on a research paper! This project is in partial fulfilment of my BSoc degree, as I keep telling you. I didn't even tell my grandmother I was coming here. She masterminded my whole training program in both college and witchery? She invested quite a lot in me? She's too old now to train someone else? ...

You say you're going to administer a delayed-action concoction on me? I will return to college and behave like a normal person for a while, then slowly begin to lose sanity? But I will expose you before that! You won't get away with this! I'll tell my professor, the college, the mental hospital and the police what you just said, what you did to me. Just you wait! ...

All those are skeptics, you say? No one will believe a schizoid, or the ravings of a once brilliant student losing touch with reality? ...

You're now emerging from the gloom of the inner room. I can now see you as clearly as I saw my grandmother in the divining mirror. So this is the real Chikanga! ...

What are you doing with that razor blade? Incisions on me? Get your assistants off me! Don't come near me, I said!

Don't touch me! ...

The Widow's Revenge

1

"Is the medicine ready?" Uncle Ndamo asked, as if to no one in particular.

"It is ready," Mrs Andaunire, Atupele's mother, answered.

It was Atupele's cue to leave the room. With a raging heart, she lifted herself heavily from the mat. The sob she stifled was not because of Pangapatha, her late husband, whom they had all helped to bury that afternoon. It was the helpless anger that these elderly people—Uncle Ndamo heading her husband's relatives and Mrs Andaunire the only person representing the widow's side—had all consented to the *kusudzula* ceremony she had to go through now.

"Be prepared for the *kusudzula* this evening," her mother had warned her.

"I thought the ceremony takes place months or even a year later."

"You know I'm managing Andaunire Enterprises alone now. I can't afford a day away from the business. I'm losing thousands as I stand here."

"How can I bury my husband in the afternoon and then go through the *kusudzula* the same evening?"

"Listen, I only came to this funeral because you are my daughter. Your father, even if he was alive, wouldn't have come. Your uncle refused to come with me even when I offered him the transport. You know the reasons why. In any case, I don't want to have to come here again, ever, even for the *kusudzula*, if you don't want to go through it today."

"Does the Ndamo side know about this?" Atupele couldn't see herself coming to Mutopa village alone at some future date even for the *sadaka*, either.

"I've told them what I told you." Her mother was firm. "I brought the medicine in anticipation for this. So be ready for the man."

Of course, the elders also knew, in fact, had already chosen which of her in-laws she was to consummate the rite with. Sigele Jika, her mother told her, as if she was telling her which man would take her shopping. Sigele Jika, the same man who had selflessly helped the couple financially in Pangapatha's last dying days. It was Sigele, sitting almost dejectedly a little way away from the male elders around the table, who had also bought the coffin and transported the body to Mutopa village in his pick-up. He had continued to be transport officer till the burial this afternoon. Now they had requested him to perform this last ceremony, too. How much can relatives ask of a man?

As she got up, Atupele did not look at the other half-dozen or so elders around the table. Her foot caught in the folds of her *chitenje*. She stumbled and held onto her mother's shoulder, sitting on the same mat as the other elderly women. Her mother did not offer to lead her outside as the other women had done at the last evening of the deceased. Atupele had been hysterical then. "My husband! Who is going to take care of the children?" she had wailed. They had trudged from the bereaved's house to join the coffin on Sigele's pick-up since the service was to be held in the little church on Mutopa Hill. In her unsteady walk to the pick-up, she had also been led by a group of supportive women.

It had been like this up to the laying of the wreaths, when she broke down and had to be half-carried away from the mound, now looking flamboyant with the multicolored flowers from relatives, friends, and colleagues.

No, no supportive woman led her outside. The last widow's rite was all her own, with the appointed man. There the women sat, unmoving and, it seemed, even unmoved by what was going to happen to her. Bowed greying heads, cupped palms under chins, legs folded to one side in the characteristic pose of the African village woman. In that pose, the trunk was always leaning to one side, lopsided. The women resolutely refused even eye contact with her.

Atupele now knew why sacrificial animals going to slaughter bleat, she thought, bleakly holding back another flood of tears as she emerged from Uncle Ndamo's house.

2

It was now quite dark outside. The fire in front of the bereaved's house was dying. Someone must stoke it before it died out entirely. Atupele looked around as if that was the most urgent thing to do. Where was everyone? There had been all night singing in and around the bereaved's house. Now it was silent. The affairs of the funeral were left with the owners of the village. She was one of the affairs of the village. Atupele continued her solitary walk to grandmother's hut. The heat and dryness of the air were still there in the air. At least it was free air outside, rather than the musty inside she had just left.

Atupele walked over uneven bare ground covered with patches of *kapinga* grass. She had walked over the same route several times since she came with the body. Attempts at making lawns and flower gardens in the village were not always successful. The results were sometimes stumbling blocks between crowded houses, kitchens, bathrooms, and even animal or chicken sheds.

She knew where Agogo's hut lay. It was where they had tried to make her eat the food they had prepared for the mourners. She couldn't eat any. In fact, she hadn't eaten anything since coming to Mutopa village. She didn't feel hungry, only drained of energy. And emotion. And even will power.

She climbed the *khonde* of Agogo's hut. It was only one step up and forward to the thin pine door. She turned the handle and entered the yawning door. It was darker here. It smelt of dry dust and ash. It held the permanent odor of a windowless hut whose only ventilation was the door. It had the same feel as her own grandmother's at Mbamba on the lakeshore.

She held out her hands in front of her to meet any objects in her progress inside. She stepped to her right, along the wall. After a few steps she bumped against a bed post. She leaned down and felt the frame all along to the very end. There was what felt like a small table beside the bed. She felt on top and brushed against a matchbox. That's better, she could at least light up the place.

The flare revealed a small tin lamp on the table. Atupele lit it and surveyed the room again. Nothing much. There was the single bed, the table, and a folding chair. A storage basket and a pot stood on one side of an empty fireplace in the center of the room. A rolled up reed mat stood near the door. There were some clothes hanging on a string strung under the rafters from one end to the other. It looked desolate.

Some of Atupele's happiest moments were spent in her own grandmother's hut at Mbamba. After the evening meal, the children would gather round her fireplace seated on the firestones, a mat, or even her bed, roasting maize or potatoes, telling stories or throwing riddles. Whenever she had done some mischief, she'd end up in her grandmother's hut. It was a place of refuge. The only place at home, in fact, she felt free. Grandmother treated her like a human being. Unformed maybe, but lovable. There Atupele would lie snuggled against her grandmother after the fire had died out. How far away it was now from that hut, and so different. Only she had come in for a necessary ritual. Necessary for whom?

"Do I have to go through all this?" Atupele had asked her mother. "I didn't go through all the initiation ceremonies as I grew up, since we lived mostly in town. Only the first and the last one. Why do I have to do this?"

"Every widow has to go through this, or else she's not free to marry again."

"Buy I don't want to marry another man. Pangapatha was everything to me. That's why I married him, even against your and father's wishes. After him, I shall remain single for the rest of my life."

"There are other reasons behind the ritual, my daughter. It's not only to set you free."

"What reasons, mother?"

"Don't start giving me headaches again, as you did when you got pregnant in school and ran away to get married. All the elders here have been through it, man or woman. All of them. They expect you to go through it too, or we're going to have a case on our hands."

"Did they *kusudzula* you too?"

"Don't you remember Uncle Mbungo coming home to collect his brother's property? That's not all he came for."

Atupele didn't know all the details. She only remembered Uncle Mbungo coming over one long afternoon. Uncle Mbungo rarely visited them even when father was alive. This time he behaved like he was a regular visitor. Her mother behaved strangely too, like a little girl again. They were like marriageable cousins. It went on like this at the meal and afterward. Then Uncle sent Atupele to buy groceries down the road. This was a two-kilometer return trip. When Atupele returned, Uncle had departed. What about the groceries? she had asked. He bought those for us, her mother had explained. Atupele went into the house to find it half-empty. Where was all the furniture? We've shared it with your father's relatives, mother said. Together with the bicycle? Of course: what are we women going to do with it? Atupele's heart sank. She didn't want to remind her mother that she was still at school. Or that they could have sold it themselves to add on to what now looked like a hard future for them financially. Atupele had kept quiet.

Of course, her mother had gone through the *kusudzula* ceremony. It had included the distribution of the deceased's property. Just like what Atupele was going through now, as custom demanded.

3

Atupele was undecided for a few moments. Should they use Agogo's bed. It was a single bed and might not withstand much agitation. The mat? It would be hard on the bare floor. She settled for Agogo's bed. It sounded outrageous but she reckoned, if the custom came from the elders, it made sense to perform it where the likes of Agogo slept. She sat on the bed dejectedly.

Atupele had not told her mother the real reason she couldn't marry again. Pangapatha had made her promise not to or else he wasn't going to write the last letter that served as the will that evening when the distribution of wealth was contested. In fact, it had been no accident that the letter was discovered among her husband's effects. Her husband had not been doing too well in the construction business. The government tenders he used to enjoy in the first republic were no longer forthcoming. He discovered it was because he was in the wrong party.

Before long, he was reduced to building petty traders' one-roomed groceries or bottle stores. His illness drained him the other way too, as he had to keep track of who the next best medicine man was. He sold his pick-up and resorted to public transport and sleeping in dingy resthouses. Atupele grew alarmed as she observed themselves getting more and more destitute. They had their own house, of course, but then there were the water and electricity bills. Four of the children were in school. One in secondary. Another joining the other next year. The last one starting next year, too. And the food and the clothes to be bought.

Meanwhile, Pangapatha grew weaker and more helpless. Atupele persuaded her husband to write a letter addressed to her.

"Do you think I'm dying?" Pangapatha had protested.

"We are all going to die, eventually," Atupele had pointed out. "Even if we live long enough, we must have a record of how we want our property to be distributed when we go."

"But I'll leave everything to you and the children."

"That's what you say, and I believe you. But your relatives won't believe me when I tell them the same thing. Look at what happened to Andilandazonse, our neighbor. The father, uncle, and brothers came in a truck to clear the house and chase her out. She was left with only the clothes on her back, a few pots and plates. Even the children went to live with their grandfather in the village. Do you want that to happen to us?"

"Do you love me?"

"You know I do."

"Will you marry another man when I'm gone?"

"I couldn't think of doing that. Why?"

"Well, then, I will write this letter only if you promise to remain single all the rest of your life. You know I love you, too."

"I promise I will do as you wish."

It was true Atupule loved her husband. She remembered the time Pangapatha came to her secondary school to do some extension work to the buildings. Somehow he had timed his trips to Mbamba trading center to coincide with her going home after school. It all started with: Do you want a lift? At first, Atupele said no. Pangapatha persisted. She gave in after a while: it was a five-or-so-kilometer walk home otherwise.

It was a straight lift in the early days. Then the journey became interrupted by stopovers at a superette in Mbamba. A drink and a packet of biscuits. It went on like this till the invitation to the lakeshore resort where Pangapatha was staying. As the saying goes, one thing led to another, till she found herself pregnant. The school couldn't keep her. Nor could her father. Her grandmother had died by this time. She joined Pangapatha at the resort, till he fulfilled his contract. She then went with him to Kamba city. Her father disowned her. Her mother relented only for the *chisamba* ceremony: You are still my daughter, I carried you inside me. I, too, had to go through the *chisamba* ceremony, she had told Atupele.

Her mother arranged the *chisamba* with other expectant women in another village. Her father didn't know, but then he died a few years later. Atupele and her mother kept loose contact with each other after her father's death.

Atupele kept her mother posted on the appearance of her grandchildren. There was Ayami after Awechete. Then Ndemile …. Her mother was rather indifferent to the additions. She only started showing concern when Atupele reported Pangapatha's deteriorating health and their doing the rounds of clinics and medicine men. Atupele was very grateful for her mother's concern, otherwise she would have had no one on her side.

4

Atupele wondered whether or not to keep the little lamp on. She blew it out decisively. This ritual should happen in darkness, she thought. It would be like the *kuchotsa fumbi*, the ritual deflowering of nubile girls after their first initiation ceremony. The *fisi* or hyena, the deflowerer, came in the night, unannounced. He performed his duties silently and departed anonymously. Only in her case she would know who it was. Even though she knew who it was she preferred not having to watch herself being violated, for that was what it amounted to.

There was a smell like singed hair when she blew the lamp out. Then she was plunged into thick darkness. The door was still open but she could not see the smoldering outside fire anymore. Perhaps it was because she had moved from light to darkness too rapidly. Her eyes had yet to adjust.

Atupele pulled the blouse over her head while seated, being careful not to bruise the sores around her wrists. She shrugged her shoulders free of the straps of the bra she was wearing. She turned it back to front. It was always difficult to unclasp it from the back. She unclasped it and let it fall on her lap. She untied the headband, too. Her straightened hair frothed out. Some of it caressed her neck, collarbones, and shoulder blades.

She untied the *chitenje* and spread it around her on the bed. There was only a *mkeka* mat on the bed. Agogo's blanket was on the string above her. In any case it would not have been decent to do it on top of Agogo's blanket. Her own *chitenje* would absorb all the mess.

Atupele stood up and hooked her thumbs on top of her pants and pulled them down. They slithered down to her ankles. She sat down again. She removed her right shoe with the big toe of the other foot. She reversed the procedure for the remaining shoe. She freed the feet from the pants by lifting them and shaking them off, careful not to bruise the sores on her ankles. She let the pants lie where they were and put her feet down again. Her bare feet felt the hard, dry mud flooring. She pushed the bra on the floor to join the pants.

Atupele was babe naked. She felt her breasts. The nipples were hard but cold. She was cold inside herself too, shrunken within her womanhood. She put her elbows on her thighs and hugged her knees together. She put her head to her knees feeling her cold breasts and tits on her cold thighs.

It was not the idea of having sex with a strange man that shattered her most. It was the fact that her mother, yes, and all those elders in that house, had planned it all for her. Yes, the fact that they had conspired that she should do it without asking for her consent that had killed something within her. Interestingly enough, *kusudzula* was one of the things the elders never told the growing girls to be on the lookout for at the initiation ceremonies. Not even at the wedding *mwambo* ceremony. That, should one of them die first, this is what was in store for the survivor.

Of course, she had heard of *kusudzula* before, but it was only hearsay. It happened to other women, not her. When Pangapatha died, it still had not entered her mind, till her mother told her to prepare for it. Then things started exploding inside her. She spent the rest of the time weeping for her husband and for herself. As she lay in the fetal position, an image of her father came to her.

She must have been six or so. She heard her father chanting in front of a bush near the garden.

Chelule, *go to sleep!*

Chelule, *go to sleep!*

Atupele thought it strange for such an elderly person to be chanting the silly song as she and her friends did in the playground. Her father was peering under the umbrella formed by the shrubbery. She wanted to see what he could see there.

"Don't come any nearer," her father warned furiously. "You'll frighten it away."

"What is it, father?" she hissed back at him.

"The *chelule* bird."

Her father was chanting to a bird in the depths of the foliage. It kept fluttering up and around from one branch to another, then drooping as if it was tired and going to sleep. It hopped up again, then drooped, as if it would fall off the branch, weary with sleep.

"*Chelule*, go to sleep!" her father chanted earnestly, if not desperately. Her father at last suddenly threw a stone he had in his hand. The bird disentangled itself from the branches and flew away to the freedom of the skies.

"What were you doing, father?"

"The *chelule* bird can be caught by chanting to it to go to sleep. If you chant long enough you can even capture it with your bare hands. Today I was not so lucky."

Atupele felt like the little *chelule* bird. The funeral songs had made her soporific. Her mind was fuzzy. She was ready to pass out and to be easy prey to the traditional customs closing upon her. She'd better not be caught napping. But how was she going to get out of this one?

5

Atupele raised her trunk, slid her arms outwards and downwards on the bed to retrieve the loose ends of her *chitenje*. She stood up slowly and wrapped herself all the way to the armpits. It felt like a shroud.

Pangapatha must have been wrapped up like she was, only more permanently. She chilled at the thought.

Perhaps, Atupele clung to a stray thought, to avoid the pain of penetration she ought to want to enjoy what was to come. After all, she reassured herself, she did not find Sigele Jika unattractive, in spite of his age. Furthermore, her husband hadn't been able to fulfil his marital obligations toward the end, as he got sicker and weaker. Perhaps the feel of a man inside her would do something positive to her, after what she had been through. It would be something of a reward to Sigele, too, after what *he* had been through to help them. She recalled her first encounter with Sigele.

It was on their return from Ngwangwa for another futile consultation with a traditional medicine man. They had stopped at Mtalika to see Dr Mitsitsi, Pangapatha's old friend. The doctor took one look at his friend and gave him a hospital bed. It was while he was admitted that Pangapatha started talking about his brother Sigele Jika, who worked in town. She phoned him at her husband's insistence. Sigele came the following morning to find her and the nurse syringing the patient. By this time Pangapatha was so weak he couldn't even clean his ears.

Atupele caught Sigele several times looking at her closely. She knew why: it was the sores on her wrists and ankles. She didn't mind the inspection. She couldn't help them anyway: her husband had given them to her. At first, it was STDs, followed by tests. Then the sores. Pretty soon, they would have to go for VCT and then they'd be on ARVs. That's what Pangapatha was afraid of. He didn't want to learn the truth. Hence all this running around from clinic to clinic to traditional medicine man covering half the country. Even Dr Mitsitsi advised them strongly to go for thorough tests at one of the big hospitals in Kamba.

They went to the big hospital. Pangapatha was admitted immediately. Atupele phoned Sigele, but the man was not responsive. She had to phone him again when Pangapatha died a few days later. He was the only person she had met who could help with the funeral arrangements. Ndamo, her father-in-law, was only a subsistence farmer in Njati district. Her own father was dead. Her mother would not go that far to help.

Sigele, strangely enough, complied. He came with his pick-up and took over the funeral arrangements.

It was in these encounters that Atupele found Sigele appealing, yes, that was the word, not attractive. The man was about her father's age, going bald, and rather flabby around the middle. It had something to do with his eyes. Something hesitant, if not restless, like a bird that had not yet decided on which branch to build its nest. Yes, that's it. Nothing furtive, but filled with wonder all the same, something that made Atupele feel as if she wanted to help him build that nest. Yes, aid him.

Then it wouldn't be fair to let him touch her. Atupele couldn't allow Sigele to … She would have to tell him the truth. About Pangapatha's death … About the sores … She could imagine the impact it would have on him, if he came, at all.

Let's break this custom, Atupele would say to him.

It's for your sake, he would respond.

My sake? It doesn't mean anything to me, just a violation of my body, that's all.

Why don't you really want to go through with it?

It's dangerous, I tell you.

Where's the danger?

It's been spreading STDs down the ages and now the deadly AIDS.

It's between consenting adults. They should know their sero-status.

Some of them don't and kill each other as a result. This kusudzula *business will wipe out families and villages. The entire nation is at risk.*

Do you know your sero-status?

I do. I'm HIV positive. (Atupele had gone for VCT while at the hospital. The man there even told her what the sores were: Kaposi's Sarcoma, he said.)

You're what? Why didn't you tell the elders this?

Do you think they'll understand? All they're interested in is for the custom to go on. I tried arguing with mother, she almost banished me.

Well, I certainly can't go through with it, now. I suspected it all along, seeing the sores all over your limbs.

I knew you knew.

What are we going to do now?

Tell them we did it.

But that'd be a lie.

Look, my husband died of AIDS, you know that. I'll be dying of AIDS pretty soon, too. Do you want to follow suit? What about your wife?

It'd be a small start, Atupele thought. Just the two of them severing the custom. Perhaps the elders would know, by and by, and the reasons why. Perhaps they would come up with a substitute rite. Something to symbolize the act without flesh meeting flesh. Perhaps.

Yes, Atupele was determined now. She would tell Sigele the truth. The elders can bury their outdated custom together with Pangapatha out there under the *nkhadzi* trees. It only starts with one or two. The rest would follow, however long it might take them.

6

Atupele shivered when she heard the rubber soles thump on the bare earth outside. The footsteps approached Agogo's hut. There was no "*Odi*," only the feet sliding through the open door. The shadow deepened the darkness in the room. Atupele wondered fleetingly if the outside fire had been stoked again. She couldn't see it from where she lay. How she could think of it at that time she couldn't fathom. Then the door was shut. It felt as though her heart was also closing against itself.

"*Alamu*," the voice reached across the void.

No answer. Atupele's arms glued her knees together where she shrank on the bed.

"*Alamu*," the form cleared its throat. Atupele jerked up. She had come to recognize Sigele's cough and clearing of the vocal passage before he spoke.

"Who are you?"

"It's Ndakulapa, in-law."

"What are you doing here?" Atupele sprang to her feet almost screaming. She trembled at the knees and slumped down again. "Where is Sigele?"

"Gone. Let me explain."

Atupele tightened her *chitenje* and the grip on it. She felt around the table for the matches. She almost crushed the flimsy box as she pulled out a stick with hands that had suddenly become nerveless. She struck once. Then again. A flare this time. She waved the flame around and saw the indistinct figure in front of her. It was not Sigele. She strangled a scream. She shook her burnt fingers to cool them. She reached out for another stick, struck it, and held it against the wick of the tin lamp. The flame almost died out with the force of being pressed down. It wavered but caught. The room was filled with a ghostly glow.

"You're not Sigele." She sobbed hysterically. The elders had cheated her again in the choice of men. All her life it was the elders deciding for her. She had been shunted around from one initiation to another, as if she was a ritual object. No one asked her what her wishes were. What she really felt inside. Now this strange man.

"I'm his older brother." Ndakulapa stepped nearer. "It's like this …."

"Stay where you are!" Atupele swallowed and choked.

Ndakulapa did not obey the instructions. He pulled the folding chair and sat down instead. He turned in the chair and faced her. Atupele's rage threatened to explode inside her. If the elders were playing around with her again like, this someone must be made to pay for it.

"Well," Atupele said limply as she lay back. "Do what you came for."

She closed her eyes. Gritted her teeth and tried to relax but couldn't. She was conscious of every movement but could not respond. She wasn't meant to. It was like this at the *kuchotsa fumbi*, too: the inability to relax and be ready for the performance.

"Your heart wasn't there," Ndakulapa said afterwards.

"It couldn't be," Atupele mumbled groggily. "It's as they say, just a ritual, isn't it? Something anyone could do or should go through to the next stage. Only it was my turn this time. Why me? Why you? As a matter of fact, I haven't even looked at you properly. I don't know you in the way I know Sigele."

"What difference does it make?" Ndakulapa had gone back to the little chair and sat down "He'd have done what I did."

"No, he wouldn't have," Atupele said, emphatically.

"You have doubts about his manhood?" Ndakulapa almost snorted.

"No, not that. He looks quite virile to me" Atupele didn't feel embarrassed to be covered only in a *chitenje* with her underclothes at her feet. In fact, she felt strangely liberated, as if she had just emerged from a cocoon. Maybe the elders were right about the rite, after all. "It's only that I'd have told him the truth. It's the truth that would have stopped him from going on with the *kusudzula* you've just done."

"What truth?"

"I'm HIV positive."

"You're what? Then why ...?"

"Exactly. It's my way of telling the elders they shouldn't have done what they did to me. Even my husband. He shouldn't have done what he did to me, at all." Maybe cocoon was not the right image. Perhaps, the *chelule* bird fluttering around in a maze of branches that were confining her, then suddenly finding an opening to escape from man's trap. This image was more appropriate.

"What's all this about? What are you getting at?"

"When I ran away with Pangapatha I imagined a world where men loved their women. Indeed, Pangapatha loved me in his own way. At first. Then came the STDs, the tests, and now this. You haven't looked at me closely have you? You only came in this morning for the burial. Well, if you had looked at me as closely, as Sigele did, you would have noticed the sores on my wrists, and ankles. But you didn't. Even when you came into this room and I lit the lamp. Sigele knew and, as you say, he's gone. Now you know why he's gone."

"You mean Sigele let me take his place knowing you had AIDS?"

"I don't know how Jikas treat each other. What I know is how my husband treated me. If the husband whom I loved killed me in this way, then I shouldn't have a conscience returning the unwanted gift back to the family that gave it to me in the first place."

"My own brother!" Ndakulapa almost choked.

"Think of me." Atupele sat upright on the bed. "My own husband. The father of my children."

"My own in-law, too." Ndakulapa didn't seem to have heard her.

"You must enjoy this, if you are the one they send to perform the ceremony."

"It's just a service to the family. Nothing personal."

"Not the way you came drooling, like a mongrel about to mount a bitch on heat."

"There are no emotions involved. Just a rite."

"No emotions? You didn't think of me and my emotions, did you? What do you think I've been through all these years, with my husband a walking corpse? Knowing what he did to other women?"

"You're transferring your husband's sins onto me."

"But, in-law, you performed the rite knowing it was somebody else's wife. Haven't you got a wife? What does she think about your specialty?"

"She, too, is a traditional woman. She believes in these rites." Ndakulapa put his elbows on his thighs, hands between his knees, and bent over.

"I want to believe in these rites, too, but not when they're killing me and killing us all in the end. If it was you who had AIDS you'd have passed it onto me the same way, right?"

"I wouldn't."

"Really? How very honest. But just think of me. What do you think I felt when you came to me? Yes, entered me ...?

"Same thing ... fulfilling a function."

"Go in peace then, in-law, and report to the elders that you have fulfilled your function. I, too, have done what was required of the widow."

Ndakulapa shuffled to his feet. He bent down to look at his trousers as if he could see the virus there already multiplying. He made a guttural sound and stepped up to Atupele as if he would squeeze her out of this world. Atupele sat unmoving throughout. Ndakulapa made another sound and slunk to the door. He opened it and stumbled down the *khonde* step. He left the door open.

After a while, Atupele roused herself from the bed. She walked on bare feet to close the door. Ndakulapa had melted into the darkness outside. Atupele wondered how the ritual would end now. The fire outside the bereaved's house had definitely gone out. She shut the door and settled back on Agogo's bed in her earlier position: elbows on thighs and bowed head in cupped hands.

A Party for the Dead

1

I was going over the guest list for the hundredth time when Sokole, a workmate and friend, walked into my open office. His corrugated forehead made me sit up.

"Mtunduwatha is dead!"

"What?!" I was paralyzed. Mtunduwatha was one of the up-and-coming young executives.

"Car accident."

It had to be a car accident. Mtunduwatha was in his mid-thirties, as healthy as they come. It was only yesterday, I had been sprinting to catch another colleague in the corridor when I bumped into him.

"Oh, so you're still healthy enough to run?" he had said, as he joined me for a few steps.

"I can marathon you to hell and back," I had joked breathlessly as I rushed past. I was a good fifteen years older than him.

"No! It can't be true!" I said hoarsely.

"I actually saw the car being towed in by the police." Sokole's shoulders convulsed.

"But I saw him yesterday afternoon, before knocking off."

"It happened last night."

"Where?"

He told me.

"What are the funeral arrangements?"

"We don't know as yet. We're waiting for the boss to tell us."

Sokole's footsteps echoed mournfully in the corridor as he walked out. I slumped in my seat.

My wife and I had both liked Mtunduwatha. We had invited his family over several times for dinner or drinks. They were coming to the party on Saturday, too.

"We'll have to cancel our party," I said despairingly to an empty office.

Suddenly the full implications of Mtunduwatha's death hit me, and I was overwhelmed by conflicting emotions.

It had taken us a long time to organize the party. I remembered the long list of guests, inclusions, exclusions, deletions, additions, arguments with my wife on doubtful names of people we didn't exactly like or know, but who for some reason or other we had to invite.

The party was going to be a major social event, with friends from all over the country meeting after long separations. We had spent a lot of money too, to make sure everyone enjoyed themselves. It was to be the party of the year.

Although it was one in a series of Christmas festivities, we had selected this particular Saturday because it was not too near Christmas to compete with others' parties. It was just close enough to Christmas to be part of the season's spirit, but far enough to be an independent event.

And here was Mtunduwatha dying on us just three days before the big occasion. Three quarters of our guests would be going to the funeral.

"Will you go to his village for the burial?" my wife sobbed, when I phoned her.

"I have to. He was like a brother."

My minor prayer had been that it wouldn't rain on Saturday, to make the party a wet, muddy affair. The house could not accommodate the more than one hundred guests. That is why I had arranged for the whole garden to be used for clusters of guests to sit around, leaving the lounge free for dancing.

My major prayer had been that my old, ailing aunt would not die during the week. She had been in and out of hospital during the past four months. I would obviously have had to cancel the party if she had died. She hadn't, but Mtunduwatha had. I had not anticipated sabotage coming from the office.

I settled down to do some phoning. I had to ring close to one hundred numbers before knocking off.

"Hello?"

"You got our invitation?"

"I've got it right in front of me. My wife and I are looking forward to …"

"Exactly. We've had to cancel it."

"What happened?"

"Mtunduwatha is dead."

Dead silence. Then, "It can't be." My reiteration.

"I know people are dying all over the place," one of them said, "and it's cruel to say it but he was one of those young men you don't imagine dying so young."

It was the same ritual for the other names. Well, with slight variations.

"I've been told already," one guest said.

"Oh?"

"He happens to be a cousin of mine, so they told me early."

The most difficult ones were those not on the phone.

"This telephone is temporarily out of order." I wondered why. Unpaid bills? Had they gone out of town and disconnected to prevent the servants from using it? How was I going to get in touch with them before Saturday? For one family, I had to leave messages in three different hotels I knew they frequented, on the off chance they would get at least one.

I drove round personally to those in town. I sent messages to others by word of mouth, or left notes. By lunch time, I was in a daze.

"He's messed up our party," I complained at table.

"Think of the mess his wife is in," my wife reminded me.

Mtunduwatha had left two kids, ten and seven, a boy and a girl.

We ate in silence. I was thinking of the kilos of pork, chicken, peanuts; liters of beer, wine, spirits, in various parts of the house.

"When are we going to eat the cake?" my youngest kid asked. We had left the huge cake on the dining table for lack of space in the kitchen.

"We can start right now," my wife said. "Otherwise it will go bad."

She unwrapped the foil. My stomach turned as I saw all the almonds and dried fruit embedded in the cake. I looked away.

"What are we going to do with all the food?"

"Put it in the freezer. It can keep for at least three months."

"We haven't got a freezer that big."

"We've got friends who can help us out."

132

"What are we going to do with it during the three months. We can't have chicken and pork every day. They'll start clucking and honking through our ears and noses within a fortnight!"

"We're still going to hold the party, aren't we?"

"The earliest I can think of is the Easter vacation. Say Good Friday?"

"I don't approve of parties on Good Friday. In any case, it's too far away. We can still have it in January."

"It's anticlimactic to hold a party after Christmas and the New Year. People are fed up with everything."

"They may be bored, but not fed up. People love parties. After all, we're asking them to come and wine, dine, and dance at our own expense."

2

We leave the house of the deceased in a very orderly manner.

It is not far to the graveyard, as we discover before long. However, it seems further as, every minute or so, brown hands stop all progress to relieve the bearers of the coffin. Some of the brown hands I recognize as belonging to guests who were supposed to be coming to our party this evening. Instead of holding wine glasses and snacks they carry the brass handles of the coffin in tight, nervous, sorrowful grip, staring gloomily ahead. Instead of swaying to the rhythm of dance music, they march the slow, measured steps of grief, with funeral hymns punctuating each step as the cortege nears the graveyard. Instead of the noisy chatter and guffaws of the inebriated, it is the sobbing, wailing, choking, nose-blowing that mix with the funereal melodies surrounding me. I shake my head again in disbelief.

Bare brown feet toast in the hot dry dust of the path. The sun is so hot even the rubber soled shoes I am wearing do not protect me. Sweat pours out of every imaginable pore. It makes me think ahead to the weekend at the lake I am taking my family to between Christmas and the New Year. Just to get away from the bouts of elation and misery we seem to be alternately wallowing in.

"What are you celebrating?" I had asked Sokole in the staff room. He was buying a round of drinks for the accountant, executive secretary, and administrative officer, all sitting at a corner table.

"We're organizing the staff Christmas party."

"I hope it's not for this Saturday. That's reserved for mine."

"Don't worry!" Sokole had grinned. "We all know about your big party. Nothing could disturb that one. This one is for next week."

"There seem to be too many parties this year."

"It's to compensate for all the funerals we've been attending lately."

We had both laughed, although it was no laughing matter. We had lost four staff members: two from mysterious causes and two in car accidents. A party or two would surely console some depressed souls.

We enter the graveyard, recently cleared of a tangle of grass and shrubs for the new inmate. I see mango, cassava, and sugarcane peels, snacks for the gravediggers, hastily scattered to disguise the fact that there had been a feast here before our arrival. It reminds me of an initiation song:

> *The* nalimvimvi *is not fat*
> *from birth.*
> *He feeds on funeral food.*

At the rate we were losing our young men, some of the regular gravediggers would be putting on as much weight as the corpulent insect of the song. *It is only the earth*, as another song goes, *that doesn't get fat from feeding on so many corpses.*

It is an extensive graveyard. The more-than-a-mile long procession is easily contained in the spaces between the mounds, concrete slabs, and passages where more bodies will eventually be buried. It is also an ancient graveyard, judging not only from some of the now indecipherable writings on the stones or crosses but also from the gnarled trunks and branches of the trees shading the graves. The mourners gratefully flee to the shade of these old trees, away from the pitiless sun. Even the reverend in his robes with his entourage retires to the nearest tree after his *dust to dust, ashes to ashes*, to wait for the mountains of earth to be returned to the hole once the coffin has been lowered.

"What are you celebrating?" my friends had asked upon receiving the invitation.

"Can't I hold a party without celebrating something?" I had kept retorting.

"Most people organizing parties these days ask their friends to contribute money first and then invite them as guests. Here you are inviting half the country to come and wine, dine, and dance for free with you. It can't just be for the fun of it."

"We haven't had a party for years. We've been dining, drinking, and dancing at other people's parties free of charge for too long. It's our turn to return the compliment."

The explanation had satisfied some but it had not convinced me. The more I had thought about it, the more I had been persuaded that I was really paying tribute to my ancestral spirits. I had not been to my father's graveyard for some time. My relatives had held a commemoration for him a few years ago, but I had been abroad. My mother had died when I had been overseas too. I had visited the subsiding earth mound three months later. The prayer that I had uttered at the graveyard had choked in my throat. Then there had been my uncle before them. And my grandmother. My kid brother, too. And little nephews and nieces. I felt that they were all out there pressuring me to do something. The party was to appease all these hungry spirits who had died before me and before their time, I realized.

But here was Mtunduwatha denying me my resolve to expiate my sins of omission. In dying, he was preventing me from sacrificing to my ancestral spirits. What right had he? If it came to that, what was he a sacrifice to? He had not died a natural death of old age. He had been in his prime. A target for sacrificial rites for the gods or the spirits. They had not wanted him to live to come to my party. They did not want me to hold my party either. What did they really want?

I remembered the carcase of the pig. Dismembered parts: trotters, snout, entrails, the disembowelled navel, lying bleeding on the plastic sheet before the butcher hacked the limbs to weigh them on the hanging scales. I imagined Mtunduwatha squashed up in the driver's seat under the bridge. His bones smashed up. Some of his limbs hacked by the metal.

They had had to remove him by cutting him out to separate him from the metal. What was he really a sacrifice to? Did he too have some sins of omission or commission to expiate?

"Shall I bring a brandy?" I remember Mtunduwatha asking me when I had handed him the invitation card. I had just laughed.

It is now time for laying the wreaths. The reverend does not spare the young widow. Her fresh wreath must grace her husband's mound until the flowers wither, droop, and in turn change to dust. She takes the wreath from one of the elderly church women. We feel her heart tearing and wrenching in its mooring. We cannot see her face; her whole head and shoulders are covered by a black veil. We see her trembling hands as they lay the wreath at the head of the mound. We feel her knees wobbling as if her legs will give way, go earthward to join her husband underneath. Luckily, she does not collapse. Her helper supports her with strong arms and carries, rather than walks, her away from the source of her anguish. She collapses at the edge of the crowd, where her supporter also sits to wait for the long procession of wreath-layers to follow her example in grief.

"We have now reached the end of the ceremony," the reverend announces after the ordeal-by-wreaths. "Before we return to the house is there anyone who would like to say something?"

No one has the heart to say anything more after all the speech-making we had at the church and the house. The reverend does not really expect any either. He asks us to return to the house for the closing rites.

3

2nd January

I resumed work today with no fanfare. I was still in a holiday mood, though, so I spent the day with the list of invited guests, phoning them to remind them of 4th January, when my postponed party would be held. I emphasized to them that the 4th was a Friday, not a Saturday, as some confused friends thought.

"Don't miss it!" I ended each chat before putting the phone down.

I firmly pushed thoughts of funerals out of my mind. I wanted to enjoy this party after all the series of funerals I had been to last year. The new year was for pleasant thoughts only.

I checked with some of the guests whether they had their favorite numbers on tape, ready for the dancing. I wanted them to enjoy the party too.

3rd January

I spent the morning out of the office collecting drinks and depositing them in the cold room at the office to stay overnight. By mid-afternoon tomorrow, they would be well chilled. I had blocks of ice ready also, just to make sure they would stay like that for the rest of the party.

I checked that everything was on schedule and in place: food, music, furniture, appetites. It would take minimum effort tomorrow to activate the whole house and garden to an all-night binge.

In the afternoon, I worked hard in the office clearing my desk. I felt a little guilty for not having been in the office in the morning. However, I felt absolved from grievous sin since I was entertaining a good three-quarters of the staff, if not the country, tomorrow. I had to make sure everything would work out this time.

I was preparing to go home at 4:45 when the shy knock of the messenger interrupted me.

"From the boss," he announced as he walked in a dropped an open memorandum on my desk.

I could not think what the boss would want at that hour, when there was the whole of tomorrow to deal with any matters concerning me. I pulled the memo towards me and sat up with a jerk as I skimmed the few lines.

MEMORIAL SERVICE

Mtunduwatha's memorial service will be held at 4 p.m. tomorrow, Friday 4th January, in the staff room. Since you were a close friend of the deceased, the staff have unanimously decided that you should do the first reading. Please accept the honor.

Signed: *S Mfitidzalimba*, Executive Secretary

I relaxed again. The service would only take an hour or so. There would still be time to revive our spirits for the conviviality in the evening.

4th January

Friday morning came with the riotous chirping of birds in the trees in the garden. Last night's rain had washed the air clean. As I opened the bedroom windows, I could smell the dew evaporating from the blades of grass and leaves in the heat of the sun rapidly rising in a cloudless sky. It was a glorious day.

I was dressing for work when the phone rang. Who could it be at this hour, before breakfast?

I lifted the receiver and said hello to the blank wall opposite.

"It's Mavuto."

I detected the agitation in my cousin's voice. My hand chilled on the receiver.

"Our aunt is dead."

Snakes Eat Mice Too!

Ndatsalapati paused. The hoe made a dull clang as he laid it alongside the edge of the hole. The handle was slippery with sweat. He looked at his hands and saw how flushed they were from the efforts of digging. They were too moist and dirty to use to wipe off his streaming face, so he used his forearms. Some of the sweat got into his eyes and he blinked rapidly for a few moments before looking down at his legs. They were buried in red brown earth. So were his thighs. The smell of dry earth slowly enveloped him and caused him mild surprise; he had so concentrated on the work that it had temporarily deadened his sense of smell. As for the heat, that was too oppressive not to register.

He glanced at the sun and decided it was too low in the sky for him to continue. Anyway, he had taken the wrong turning. It was only his stubbornness that had made him go on for the last thirty minutes after realizing the mistake. Sweat ran in rivulets down his chest. The downy hair was matted and mixed with earth, and stuck to his skin. He grunted as he grabbed the edge of the pit and levered himself up on legs that had gone numb. He felt dizzy and feverish as he crouched like a frog to survey his labor. The dizzy spell passed in a moment, his eyes cleared, and he swore at length to see the devastation he had caused to his own garden. He stood up.

The mole he had been digging for had tunneled erratically across a quarter of the garden. And the ridges Ndatsalapati had made a few weeks before were now broken in parts. He had planted some maize last week, after the *mkokalupsya*, the rain that washes away the ashes. Moles were voracious eaters. If he did not catch this one before the shoots broke through the earth, the whole maize patch would be filled with more ridges where the little beast would be hunting for its food. Several molehills would spring up in no time. The whole area would be turned upside down. The roots of the young seeds would be gnawed away and the plants would wilt and die altogether.

He knew where the mole had first entered the garden. The large hill at the side of the maize patch told him only part of the story. That was where Ndatsalapati had started to dig. He knew also that the whole story depended on how long the animal had been there. If it was as much as even a week, then he had a long dig ahead of him. He knew moles very well. They could construct quite a complicated network of burrows: horizontal shafts and vertical. The surface ridges were only superficial highways used for hunting and collecting. The black, yellow and red hills he saw around him indicated that there were different levels and systems where the mole was digging deeper and deeper underground. It seemed the little beast aimed to make his garden a permanent home. Well, he would show him. Tomorrow, he would dig from the other side of the field. He knew the mole would not abandon the place. The sounds of digging would have signaled to the occupant that danger was approaching and the mole would have retired to its deepest and innermost retreat, from which it would not budge until found. A mole is not an overland traveler.

What galled Ndatsalapati most was that he had not taken into account the signs the mole had left to tell him roughly where he would be at a given moment. A mole could live in two or more territories with tunnels connecting the homes. It could abandon one area and live in another. The color of the soil and the freshness of the hills were one indication. The other was the smoothness of the tunnels. Frequent passage polished the tunnels so smooth that there would be no roots whatever growing across the hole, or any other obstacles. The part Ndatsalapati had dug had not told him much - that was the reason he had persisted in starting from that side. Also because he thought the tunnels did not point directly into the garden.

Yes, tomorrow he would start from the other side. Ndatsalapati shouldered his hoe and took the path that led back to his village. He did not bother to plug the hole with a stone. The mole would be there tomorrow, next week, next month, until it was killed in fact. He knew moles; one time he had tried a surface trap at the mouth of a molehill he had found near his home. The cunning animal had just tunneled round it and gone on the other side, to do more mischief or to mate with its fellows. He'd heard the story that moles only came out to mate or hunt food. Anyway, he knew that the destroyer of his garden lived alone. Moles never lived in pairs except during the breeding season, and that was only a temporary truce. Most of the time, they fought their fellows to death. They hated competition so much and defended their territory against other members of the same species so violently. Except maybe their immediate family.

Strange animals, Ndatsalapati thought, to be so aggressive and quarrelsome, and only come together to mate. He lived alone himself; the only difference was that he did not have any partner to mate with. His wife had died years ago, in childbirth. That was to have been their first child, but it had not even bothered to see the light of day.

Ndatsalapati shivered again feverishly. He felt cold, even though the sun was still above the horizon.

The most favorable time to destroy moles was before they started to breed. If you let them mate and breed, the whole area would be invaded by moles in no time, and famine would come as a matter of course. Moles could bring starvation to a whole village.

Ndatsalapati had stopped to allow the dizzy spell to pass. He resumed walking when he felt better, and removed some remaining particles of caked earth from his body. He was wearing a pair of old shorts, while the rest of the body was bare. The hoe handle over his shoulder rubbed the downy hair on his chest. The calloused feet padded faintly in the early evening. The sun threw a distorted shadow that crept in a grotesque dance over the grass and shrubs he passed.

His wife's people had buried her grudgingly. At her funeral, many could not suppress their reluctance and indignation. Ndatsalapati had caught whispers about *mfumba* in the maize garden, the magic potion that ensured the owner had high yields every year; muttering about his *ndondocha*, those zombies which were nephews and nieces cut short in their youth and imprisoned to a half-life-half-death existence in the granaries, to ensure that the grain store would never diminish; growls about the *msendawana* he kept in the sleeping hut to ensure prosperity reigned in the house; rumblings about the mice he caught to feed his zombies at night; half-suppressed laughs at the story of how, one time, his stock of mice had gone and the people could not sleep for the wailing all night of the hungry zombies in the granary, accompanied by the hooting of owls on the roof tops. He had borne all this.

His wife's people had thought he would return to his home village after that. He had not. Nor did he show any signs of doing so. It was strange, they said. He could only stay on if he was interested in taking another wife in the village, or if the chief appointed a woman willing to live with him. No initiative was taken in this direction. It was clear they did not want him in their village.

People passing close to his hut at night said they sometimes heard voices holding earnest conversations inside. An entreating male voice, obviously the man's, was easy to identify. The other, accusing, was female, and strangely enough it resembled that of his dead wife. They could not be sure, but then no one could mistake the voice of Mtunduwatha when she was alive. Bold people barged into Ndatsalapati's hut a few times. They had found only the man sitting alone inside. When asked who he had with him, his only answer was that he had been talking to himself. If they did not believe it, why did they not look around? True enough, there was nowhere anybody could hide. They saw only stacks and stacks of mice drying on spits above the fireplace.

Sometimes, people heard low singing to the accompaniment of clapping and stamping of feet, and they wondered what Ndatsalapati could be singing and dancing for at that time of night. Maybe he was entertaining his zombies! The song was familiar. They had heard it often enough from the man and his wife when she was alive, and they had gone out beer drinking together. It was one of the funeral dirges, and not a drinking song at all!

> *The people coming to the grave now*
> *Are coming with all their wealth*
> *Yet we came here without even a mat!*

Husband and wife always came back chattering like children and playfully going at each other like young lovers. They disappeared into the hut to sing uproariously before they fell silent for the night. And people wondered what strange memories haunted Ndatsalapati, to sing the song again, alone and so mournfully. Next morning, he would not be seen in the village. He would return in the evening. And when asked where he had been, he would grunt: hunting mice. Sure enough, the large bundle he would be carrying was proof of this. They let him be, shaking their heads at this strange passion for mice when everyone else was changing their diet from potato or pumpkin leaves to flying ants, now that the rains were here.

Not that he did not want to vary his diet. He had dug a lot of anthills around the village to collect flying ants. He had often been fascinated by the complicated system of chambers and staircases the ants built for themselves. It had always reminded him of molehills' shafts and tunnels. But that was before his wife had died. Now, no one could bring him near an anthill, let alone make him eat any flying ants. He had not told the people, but his wife's last request had been to be buried under an anthill. Which she had not been.

Ndatsalapati took the hoe off his shoulder and leaned it against the wall in front of his hut. He looked about him. The village was as usual minding its own business and giving the hut a wide berth. He pulled the door lever toward him, twisted it round in a semi-circle. He caught the grass door with one hand before it fell inward. He laid the stopper on the floor and shifted the door sideways to lean against the wall inside. Rats and cockroaches scuttled rapidly out of sight into nooks and crannies. The *chwi! chwi!* of newly born rats in their nests under the eaves were silenced as Ndatsalapati moved about in the gloomy interior.

The oppressive odor of mice hung in the air. He did not know what to do about the rats. His wife had kept three cats. They had disappeared on her death. The two he had bought after that he found dead under the granary one day. The last one he bought he found hanging under a *mkuyu* tree on the outskirts of the village. He did not keep any more after that. Now the rats ate his food, even fed on the mice he had caught in the bush and dried over the fireplace. They gnawed holes in the baskets and gourds where he preserved his planting seeds. They gnawed at him in his sleep. They ate anything they could get their teeth into, even his hoes. The food they could not carry away to their holes and nests, they excreted or urinated on. He had traps all round the hut and near the granaries, but gave up getting up at night to reset them after they had been sprung. One of his duties first thing in the morning and in the evening when he returned from the fields was to collect the corpses in a basket and throw them in the rubbish pit.

Ndatsalapati was making the rounds of the traps in the hut, basket in hand, when he saw the long tail of a snake wriggling under the trap near his sleeping place. It was still alive. He straightened up quickly and fetched the hoe from outside. He simply cut the snake in two. The free end convulsed for a few moments and was still. He was not sure about the other end. He went outside again and found a forked stick, and pinioned the end that was sticking out. One hand held the stick while with the other he levered the trap up with the hoe. The rest was still. He scraped the two ends of the snake onto the hoe and took them outside.

The sun had sunk over the horizon but there was still light enough to see what type of snake it was. The shimmering spots and stripes on the back were unmistakable: it was *njokandala*. It was not fully grown as yet. Its bulging stomach told him it had fed on rats before being caught in the trap. Ndatsalapati shivered again violently. His fever was coming back. He quickly went and threw the snake in the pit. He went inside and lit a fire. He warmed himself over it as it caught on. When he felt better, he finished his collection. He inspected the brown and yellow corpses that lay twisted and broken in the basket, with their incisors jutting out as if they had been snapping at the bait before death. He growled at them, lifted the basket, went outside, and threw the rats on top of the snake.

Night was approaching swiftly, so Ndatsalapati started preparing his meal. He went to the basket of flour and brought it near the fireplace. He removed a few pellets of rat dung he found on the surface. He filled a pot with some water and started making some *nsima*. As the porridge started plopping, he straightened up and reached for the mouse rack above him. He took four from the spit and put them on a plate. He finished making the *nsima* and settled down to eat.

He could see the pig-like snouts of the rats and their gleaming eyes peeping down at him from the space between the roof and the wall. He dared them to come down. He wondered mirthlessly why he bothered to go and dig for *kapeta*, *pida*, *dugu*, or *phanya* when there were these others he could very easily catch and eat. Only he could not eat rats. He enjoyed his meal, crunching the small bones of the mice with relish. He glanced at the shadow he cast on the walls and it reminded him of a big rat sitting upright. When he finished eating, the shadow straightened up and went to the other wall, where it crouched among the baskets and gourds. He put the plates in the pot he had prepared the *nsima* in, and filled it up with water. There they would stay until morning. Maybe some rats would help him clean some pieces away.

He went back to the fireplace after shutting the door, and rolled himself a *bunaya*. He smoked quietly for some minutes, listening to the night noises. The hooting of an owl nearby was punctuated by the piercing cry of a *namame* in the distance. The village had settled down to sleep. He scratched a flea from his armpit and looked drowsily at his sleeping place. It had been a hard day, and tomorrow might prove to be even more trying. He added more wood to the fire and stretched himself out. The light made the images melt eerily one into another. He could see the rats coming out in full force from their hiding places, watching and waiting for him to drop his vigilance. All around him were eyes, yellow, green, golden. They could do their worst ... Tomorrow he would kill some more of their brethren ... Tomorrow ... He scratched his armpit again ... awful ticks ... Tomorrow ... He was feeling feverish again ... He would catch the mole ...

Tomorrow -

My husband!

Please not tonight.

My husband!

Can't you allow me some rest, Mtunduwatha?

I am still in the graveyard!

How can I tell your people to bury you under an anthill?

They are my people. They will not deny me my last request.

They will say you are a witch.

I am beyond all that.

I am still with them.

Not for long.

Leave me alone.

I came to warn you.

Haven't you been doing that all these years?

This time, it's you, my husband.
That's not news.
Listen to me, my husband! It's the mole!
I am going to get it tomorrow.
It will be your last.
Go away. I am tired.

When Ndatsalapati woke up the next morning, the fever had gone. It was still early and he could hear the tailorbird cry: *Get to work! Take your hoe!* He got up, feeling strangely refreshed, although there were a few rat bites on his feet. He opened the door and the hut lightened. He collected another basketful of rats and went to dump them in the pit. He did not find the rats he had thrown there last night. Nor the snake. Maybe cats had dragged them away in the night, or owls. He usually found pellets of excrement which could only come from one or the other. The owls swallowed them, the cats tore at them.

Ndatsalapati took the empty basket round the house to the other traps. Some of the rats had died violently. The slabs of the stone traps crushed their bodies and the entrails burst open to reveal pellets of unreleased excrement or the bodies of unborn little ones. He was fascinated by the unborn ones, their bodies fully formed, and wondered how they would have behaved if they had been allowed to live. Most certainly they would have taken after their kind. This thought made him glad they had not lived to torment him.

He went to the traps under the maize granary. The collection increased. The rats had made another hole in the bamboo works, which meant he would have to repair it again. He did not know how many families lived in the granary. Probably more than in the groundnut store, which was not so large. He shuddered at the thought of how many there could be in all, round his hut and inside. He was inspecting the new hole when he heard an unfriendly hiss near his left leg. He sprang back a few feet and looked wildly under the granary. There it was with its stomach bulging. It had beaten him to his victims and was too overfed to move quickly. He heaved a sigh of relief. If it had not been so lethargic, he would not have known what had bitten him. Death was usually instantaneous. It was a *njokandala* again. A grown-up this time, and it had swallowed two rats.

Ndatsalapati took a long stick and beat the snake's head to a pulp. The snake made a few ineffectual lunges at him, but within a few minutes it was only its tail that wriggled to and fro. He took the body on the end of the stick and dumped it in the rubbish pit. Maybe a cat or an owl would find it there.

As Ndasalapati shut the door and shouldered his hoe, he wondered. The *njokandala* was a rare type of snake, and people had been known to die without seeing one. And those who did thanked themselves for not having seen one. It was an ominous snake, which could bring either bad or good luck. Seeing two within so short a time could only mean one thing: he was going to get his mole today. He squared his shoulders and took the path that led to his maize garden. He passed a few women carrying water pots on the way, but he did not exchange any greetings with them. They paused and stared at his broad, bare back as he passed them, the odor of mice going with him. He was a strange one, that one.

Ndatsalapati did not know what they thought of him. He was sure if he cared to find out about them, they would prove to be more peculiar than they made him out to be. A *nalikukuti* snake near the path made him jump back and take a circuitous route to his garden. He was sure he was not going back home by that path. A man had told a *nalikukuti* one morning: If you want to fight, wait for me here until I get back. Sure enough, he had found the snake waiting for him exactly where he had left it, although by that time it was late in the afternoon.

There were more bushes and trees along the path he took. All round him was dead silence. Ndatsalapati cast glances around him, instinctively looking for mouse tracks in the undergrowth. You could recognize them by their swept look, made by frequent running to and fro. Sometimes you could see the tracks marked by their droppings. He stopped near a grassy patch, put the hoe down, and bent over a hole. He was on all fours as, with one hand, he parted the grass to have a closer look. His nostrils flared as he peered down. It was not a live hole. There were too many grass roots obstructing the entrance. He was straightening up, disappointed, when he heard a *mkuta* bird call high up in a tree:

> *Mother died in a mouse trap!*
> *She said huh! huh! huh!*

The song was repeated over and over again. It had started suddenly, with that quiet, plaintive, haunting quality which sent a chill through him. It was like the hooting of an owl at midnight, when one was passing a graveyard: a deathly-sad song. He walked away with some trepidation.

Ndatsalapati thought he was in luck as he saw the soil erupting on top of one of the molehills. It meant the mole was this side of the garden, not where he had started to dig yesterday. It also meant the mole was near the surface. With a beating heart, he skirted the area, inspecting the other hills to see which direction the mole was taking. But they all looked the same and the mole could be heading anywhere. Cutting it off would be futile. He would have to start with the one the mole was at. Ndatsalapati tiptoed toward the hill. He crouched on his haunches, the hoe-handle held at the ready, and timed the eruptions. When it was right, he brought the handle down swiftly. There was a dull thud and Ndatsalapati quickly reversed the hoe and started digging furiously. If he had stunned the mole, he would find it immediately under the hill. A few minutes of grunting and panting found him at the nest. It was filled with newly born moles, almost hairless, their eyes still closed, and their tiny pink hands curled to their pale chests. The mother lay inert in the main tunnel.

"I've got you at last!" he growled wrathfully, as he took her by her tail and thumped her head repeatedly against the hoe-handle. A little blood oozed out of the crushed skull and stained the handle.

"I got your mole, Mtunduwatha!" he gloated, dangling the lifeless form by the tail.

He sat down to inspect the nest again. The molehill was actually an old anthill, as was revealed when he removed the hoe. He had broken open more cavities and stairways. Now, now if only his wife were buried here, maybe she would leave him alone. He noticed that he had cut right through the nest, and some of the young ones were sliced open. A few were wriggling feebly about. He was stretching out his hand towards these when he noticed the shimmering, golden spots and stripes of the *njokandala* at the edge of the pit.

"Mayo!" Ndatsalapati cried out as it struck. He writhed for a few moments, clutching at his hairy chest, and fell back into the pit. His lips peeled and contorted his face in a ghastly grin. He went rigid.

Burial at Your Own Risk

I was in the middle of my Sunday lunch when the phone rang. My wife answered it, since she had finished hers, being a faster eater. I wondered who it was at this time.

"It's Alinafe," she shouted across the sitting room. "She wants to talk to you."

Alinafe's my sister, living with her husband in Blantyre She rarely phones, so it must be serious, I thought as I went through to the hallway to take her call.

"We've just got a phone call from Uncle Mwatitha in Mulanje. Zinenani is there with them."

"But I thought she'd been admitted into the hospital here in Zomba?"

"Apparently she left the hospital on Thursday without permission and got onto a bus for Mulanje."

"She left home a week ago without saying goodbye to anyone either. No one knew she'd been admitted until Wednesday. So what's the problem now?"

"They want you to go and pick her up and bring her back home to Zomba."

"What?!" I spluttered.

"Uncle has already got two patients in the house: his wife and daughter. He says he can't cope with a third one."

"But ... but ...," I still couldn't figure it out. "There are people in Mulanje. You are nearer to Mulanje than me here."

"You know uncle is too poor to hire transport all the way from Mulanje to Zomba. We can't afford it, either. Masautso has been in and out of hospital the past three months. Each time he's had to have a minor operation. We are even considering taking him down to South Africa to see a specialist. You're the only one who can help."

That's just not true, I thought. We had two brothers in Blantyre, one, Atani, a pensioner, the other, Fatsani, a junior accountant. Between the three of them, surely they could organize transport from Blantyre, just an hour and a half from Mulanje. But they didn't have that kind of money. Zinenani's close relatives, Nankhoma, a younger sister, and her husband, lived in the village, but between them they could not even find enough money to hire a bicycle for five kilometers. Mulanje must be at least 130 kilometers from Zomba. Zinenani's other brother was in Lilongwe, close to 300 kilometers in the other direction.

From their point of view, I was indeed the only one who could help them. I was in a managerial position, earning a fat salary. I lived in a posh, low-destiny housing area. I had a car. It made sense.

"I've been making too many trips to Blantyre, lately. Friday I was there. Yesterday I was there. I was supposed to go again today, but I couldn't make it, so I just canceled the trip. Now it's already after noon, I can't possibly make the journey through Blantyre to Mulanje and back. Tell them to put her on a bus."

"She's too sick to take the bus."

"If she managed to take the bus last Thursday, all alone, and even change in Blantyre, she can't be that sick. Iphani, her younger brother, followed her to Mulanje, he can bring her back with him."

"What shall I tell them in Mulanje? They're waiting at the police station for an answer to be relayed to them in the village."

"I think Zinenani behaved irresponsibly, leaving home without anyone knowing, leaving hospital without being discharged, and planting herself at uncle's without an invitation."

"What shall I tell them?" The question clattered again in my ear.

"Tell them," I said firmly, "I can't come, and to put her on the bus with Iphani."

I hung up wearily and went back to my cold lunch. It was true. I had spent two days of the weekend in Blantyre. I was tired. I couldn't go today, mostly because I was exhausted, and although I really should have been in Blantyre working on the project again today, one can only do so much, and I had to work all week, too.

The lunch had become tasteless, I pecked at the stewed chicken, boiled potatoes and turnip greens for a few more minutes, and about to give up, when the phone rang again. My wife answered again.

"It's Alinafe again!"

This time I was really angry. If they expected me to change my mind so soon after rejecting their unreasonable request, they had another thing coming. I could not be used as an ambulance for wayward patients.

"Zinenani's dead!" Alinafe said simply.

"What?!" I almost choked

"When I rang Mulanje, they told me that since they'd contacted me a message had come through to tell them that the patient had died."

"But that's impossible!" I don't know why I said it.

"The question now is, where should she be buried?"

I reeled at the implications of Zinenani's dying in Mulanje on Uncle Mwatitha. The practical realities were enormous.

"They want ME to tell them the answer?"

"You don't have to answer it alone." She was being tactful. "They want you to go to the village, tell them the news, discuss it with them, and phone me again to relay the decision. They'll be waiting at the police station to hear from me."

"I see," was all I could say as I saw the rest of Sunday, and Monday, and maybe beyond, overfilled with phone calls to numerous relatives in other districts and personal visits to village relatives without phones. All these were merely preliminaries to the practical questions of a coffin and payment for it, funeral services, and contacting church officials.

When my uncle died last year, I had to do everything myself. The boys from the village got me up early in the morning to tell me the news, bringing with them a piece of rope to indicate the length (or is it the height?) of the deceased for the coffin. I got the hint. I started phoning sometime after breakfast, to give my other relatives time to get to their offices, since they did not have phones at home. Mid-morning, I contacted my own place of work, to have the carpentry section make a coffin.

"Which reverend," I had asked my cousins, "usually officiated in my father's village?" I had two villages, you see: my father's and my mother's, within a ten-kilometer radius of each other, my work place, and my institutional house in town. So any funeral, illness, birth, etc., reached me first, to be relayed onward.

"There's a problem here," the spokesman hesitated. "Father was not a Christian. He hasn't been one since most of us were born, so all the reverends, elders, and church women have refused to give him a Christian burial."

"Is that so?" I was angry at the injustice of it all. "Who usually officiated anyway?" They told me. I drove round to the church elder's home. He was out in the gardens. I said I could wait. They sent for him. When he came, an hour later, we had a long palaver.

"Your uncle," he kept telling me, "was a stubborn man. We discussed his coming back into the fold several times. In fact, we quarreled over it. And the last time, he said, 'If the old Indian rupee that was the currency in the country in the colonial days is brought back into circulation, then and only then will I come back into the fold'."

That sounded like my uncle all right.

"But," I persisted, "he's now dead. You cannot deny him the dignity of a Christian burial."

"Your uncle …"

"Look, he was not just an ordinary person. He was also the village headman. You can't just throw him into a grave like a dog."

"Then," said the elder, "let the other village headmen bury him. They have their own rituals for headmen, chiefs, or kings, which we churchmen cannot participate in."

It was agonizing to think what the suggestion meant. My uncle had drowned. The police had fished him out. He had already been in the mortuary without refrigeration for more than twenty-four hours. I had to pull several strings to get a post-mortem performed before the afternoon, which was their usual time. Sending delegations to the group village headman, then the chief after that, and for both to come in person or to send deputations, would take more than forty-eight hours.

The arrival of the coffin decided everyone. They put him in the coffin, said one prayer, led by the same church elder—that's all he could spare—and sent my uncle off. And that's how we buried him.

I shuddered to think what I would have to go through with Zinenani now. She was no practicing Christian either.

I drove to the village and parked by my niece Nankhoma's house, a two-roomed wattle-and-daub badly in need of re-roofing. Within two minutes, the car and I were surrounded by a swarm of kids in various tattered modes of dress or undress. One thing with my mother's village is that it is full of these kids, unmarried teenage girls, and elderly folk. The men are out in towns or dead and buried. I can never keep track of who is whose kid or father. We only meet at funerals or weddings. The latter are extremely rare, since all the men do is come, impregnate, depart. It does not matter if it's a member of the same village or an outsider. The village has become a depository or manufactory of kids. Unclaimed kids at that. Each time I come for a visit, I go through the same sense of helplessness or futility of trying to account for this or that kid. Although my little cousins and nieces once or twice removed never tire of coming to visit me in town to show me, they say, their newborn. This means parting with some money and other gifts in kind, for the little one. Where is the father? Oh, we'll come with him on our next visit. The next time, they still come alone, but this time to show me how much the little one has grown, and how well he can now play with the cousins. My kids, that is.

"Is it well with you, uncle?" was Nankhoma's greeting.

"No, it is not. I bring bad news. Zinenani has died in Mulanje."

Sniff, sob, wail. Within minutes, I was surrounded by women wailing at the top of their voices, even before they were told who had died. There was a catch in my throat. I never have been able to remain unmoved by the sound of women mourning, however many funerals I attend. It is a pity that Christian funerals put a damper on this spontaneous expression of grief. This is a Christian funeral, they say, so all the grief will be expressed in hymn and prayer. And so we go through, almost mechanically, to sing hymn number so-and-so after a reading from the Book of such-and-such, grief simmering under the mouthful of gulps for air to sing the next verse or read the next line.

"I got a phone call," I began again after the women had quietened. They had now been joined by their elderly menfolk. We sat on the grass under the mango tree. One woman sat on the *khonde*, near Nankhoma, suckling a little one. She had her whole chest bare, with the child's head

154

moving from one succulent breast to the other. She wasn't paying any attention to what was happening. She was just sniffing and sobbing.

"They asked us," I came to the practical issue, "to tell them what they should do with the body."

"They should send her back to us," Nankhoma opined. "She'll be buried here. This is her home."

I winced at the suggestion. I thought too much grief had clouded rationality. I dared not say anything yet, lest they accuse me of unduly influencing them.

"I think," mumbled an old woman, "she should be buried where she is."

I warmed to this suggestion, before I heard the reason.

"What was it," continued the crone, "that made her leave her village, go to the hospital, leave the hospital, take two buses to Mulanje? The spirits of the dead were calling her."

"What spirits, mother?" Pilira, a cousin, asked. "The spirits of her ancestors are here at home."

"You have short memories," the crone said. "You forget that Zinenani is not the first one to die in Mulanje. Ndakulapa, her aunt, went to Mwatitha in her illness, too. She died there. They buried her there. No one complained. Years later, Ndayesa, the leper, her son, followed his mother to die in Mulanje. These are the spirits that beckoned to Zinenani. 'Come,' they said, 'come and die here. You will lie by our sides'."

"But those are only two spirits."

"Two is more than enough for yearning spirits. Just think, before she went into hospital, she started selling most of her belongings. When the illness got too much, she went alone to the hospital and, in her sickness, managed to get out again, catch two buses to Mulanje. All within a week. It is only the power of the spirits that could have helped her all along."

Many of the older folk agreed with the faultless logic of the grandmother. They nodded between sobs. I figured it was time I added the practical dimension to burial in Mulanje.

"We should also think of the expenses involved. Hiring a truck from Mulanje to Zomba will cost hundreds. The last time we hired a lorry for such purposes, it cost us three hundred, and that was only from Blantyre to Zomba. From Mulanje, it'll come to nearly eight or nine hundred, if not a thousand.

The last time we had hired transport for my teenage nephew's funeral, bringing the body from Blantyre to Zomba. I had footed three quarters of the bill. His father and aunt, my brothers and sisters, had paid the rest. They came home and I provided the accommodation and subsistence too, until the shaving ceremony. I even had to provide the money for the return trip for some of them, including the boy's mother, my sister, since she's a divorcee.

Zinenani, the lately dead, was another divorcee. We didn't know where her husband was. Not that he would have cared or come even if he had known.

"Then it is up to us," one of the men volunteered, "to go to Mulanje."

There was a chorus of agreement. That was the only thing to do.

"I leave it up to you," I got up, "to decide who is to go. It is important for some to leave today, to help at the wake tonight. I shall leave tomorrow, mid-morning, with Thokozani and Ndilipo, to join them in Mulanje. Now I have to go home and phone back that we'll be with them tomorrow."

I left them there. Before going back to town, I drove out to Likale, where Thokozani, my other sister, worked. She wasn't there. She had gone to a funeral. I left a message. There was another phone message when I got home. Ndilipo, my brother from Santhe, had phoned to enquire about the funeral arrangements. The return call was straightforward: Mulanje, and could I give him a lift, he had no money for transport. No problem, I said. I had anticipated that.

"They have decided," I phoned Alinafe again, "to bury Zinenani in Mulanje."

"That was wise. It's less expensive."

"Tell Uncle Mwatitha to have the coffin made. We'll discuss the finances tomorrow. And to start on the grave—we might be late. And we really want the burial to be tomorrow. Some of us can't stay overnight."

Alinafe said she would convey the message.

I had several relatives in other districts on the phone, so I resumed phoning. A few were at home. Some had had their phones disconnected, other lines greeted me with engaged tones each time. I was in the middle of these attempts when Yaya arrived with Mphatso, her six-year-old boy, Chifundo, her nine-month-old boy, and a very young nanny.

"I thought I should pay you a surprise visit."

"Well," I responded, "it saves me a trip."

"Were you coming to visit me?"

"Yes." I came straight to the point. "Aunt Zinenani is dead."

Sob, sniff. Oh, please, not another wail. We'll have the whole neighborhood coming in the whole evening. We might even have another wake here, as well as Mulanje. She contained herself. I explained the circumstances.

"Can I come with you? I don't have enough money for transport."

"Sure," I said. "That makes a full car, then."

"It's a long time," she said after she had settled herself. "I missed aunt, and Mphatso here wanted so much to play with Dalitso. A day never passes without his mentioning his name."

"Chifundo has really grown, hasn't he?" I remarked unenthusiastically. "How many teeth has he got now?"

"Smile, Chifundo. Let uncle count your teeth!"

"Where's his father? I don't believe I've met him yet."

"He's always on the road. He goes out so often. Today I told him, 'Since you go out alone, I'll do the same. Just to show you that I can go out alone too. I do have people to go to, you know.' So here I am. Well, here we are."

I really had not met the father of the second child. Yaya had come with her first husband after Mphatso's birth, and that was the last I heard of him. He disappeared without explanation or trace. Yaya took this to be a sign of divorce and took on the other man.

"That's good," I replied. "He should know that he married an independent thinker."

Yaya had been coming to our house regularly since her secondary school days. I had not only paid her school fees, I had looked after her during the holidays. We had thought living in town, surrounded by books and all the modern amenities, would encourage her to work harder. She was such a slow learner.

"Why don't you do what other people do?" Her father had stopped me for a lift one time, reeking of *kachasu*, the local gin.

"And what's that?"

"They take one or two of their little nephews or nieces or cousins to live with them. They see to their education at least through secondary school."

"I see." I could hardly keep myself from exploding.

This is unfair, I thought. I've just finished paying school fees (including boarding fees) for one of my elder brother's sons. I'm doing the same for another nephew on my father's side, and even buying clothes for him, since both his parents are handicapped. They, too, sent a message through their son: Could I add to their funds for buying fertilizer? They were five bags short. I told them, no: My commitment to them is paying for the upkeep and education of one of their sons only.

Anyway, Yaya only completed two years of secondary school from under our roof. When she failed the Junior Certificate exams, she first went to typing school and then got a job as a copy typist, got pregnant, married, divorced, produced children by different men. All the same, she still kept in touch with us. And here she was eating afternoon snacks, drinking tea, her kids playing with ours, the ones that are not in boarding school, that is. Yaya's house-girl, she couldn't have been more than thirteen, joined in the fun, now and again running to get the mop and wipe up after Chifundo.

"Shall I drop you at home?" I asked Yaya. It was almost evening. "Since I'll be away all tomorrow, I want to sort out one or two things in the office today. I'll drop you on the way."

"Oh, how kind," Yaya enthused. "I think we'd better make it a point to come earlier next time."

I left it up to my wife to work out the details of that one. Sometimes I don't trust myself to talk.

When I dropped Yaya and her entourage, I made her promise to be ready by ten o'clock because I didn't want to be too late for the burial. It was more than two hours to Mulanje, and I really wanted to be back in Zomba before dark, if all went well.

***

Nankhoma was in the sitting room when I got up on Monday. She had brought her in-law and baby. I greeted them with some surprise.

"I don't have the bus fare," she began, "so I thought I should just join you. Since no one else in the village is going to the funeral, for the same reason, my in-law thought I shouldn't go alone. There are only the two of us."

"But, as I explained yesterday, I am also picking up my sister, brother, and now Yaya. The car can only take five adults. I have room for one of you, but not both. Your in-law will have to stay behind."

They conferred in whispers. I went to the dining room to have breakfast. I learnt that my visitors had already had theirs. They must have come in quite early.

"In-law will stay behind," Nankhoma reported later. "She'll be looking after Zinenani's property and my place, too. There are only kids left, now that my brother's in Mulanje. Anything can happen, if both of us are away."

Since I had to pick up Thokozani from Likale, and my mother's village was halfway, I took both of them with me. It would be straight to Mulanje after that.

I found three other women waiting by the roadside when I was dropping Nankhoma's in-law.

"We just want you to drop us at the bus depot. We'll take the bus."

I complied uncomprehendingly. I thought Nankhoma, her in-law, and the rest of the relatives in the village had agreed last night on who was going. It didn't matter, though; it might be a recent development. I drove on to Likale, picked up my sister, and was almost back in town when I realized I should clear up a possible misapprehension.

"I presume that all three of you have got the return fares?"

"No! We thought you'd give us the money."

"What?"

"Well, since we can't go in your car, we concluded that you would pay the fares."

"I can't. I'll drop you in town to make your way back home."

"The spirits will laugh at us," Pilira protested. "We can't return without getting to the funeral."

"Will the spirits laugh at me for running around and phoning all day yesterday, putting in petrol for the return trip to Mulanje, paying for the coffin and other expenses there? Will they?"

I relented in town.

"If you decide amongst the three of you who is the best representative, I can take ONE of you instead of Yaya."

Conferring in whispers again. In order of seniority, Yaya was dispensable. She was not essential to the rituals in Mulanje.

"I'll go," announced Pilira. She was a playmate of the deceased.

I gave the other women the fares to get back to the village. There was only one more stop before leaving town. Yaya was waiting for us, was very understanding, and accepted her dethronement. The stop in Santhe didn't take long. Ndilipo was ready.

We made good time to Limbe, in spite of the full load. I stopped to check the tire pressure. Last Friday I had driven on 200 all round when I had specifically asked for 250. Now that I had a carload, I wanted it at 280, the manual's specification.

It was hot, and we spoke very little after leaving Limbe. There were occasional comments on how withered the maize looked without the rains. It was yellowing and wilting all around us, as we sped along the narrow, pot-hole-dotted road to Thyolo and beyond to Luchenza.

I had brought a whole bunch of bananas from home. We had planted virtually a hedgerow of a variety of banana trees, which we ate from all year round.

"We'd better eat these now." I hefted the bunch from between my brother's feet. He was in front beside me. The women were behind. "We might not have anything to eat at the funeral."

"This was a good idea." Ndilipo broke off two. "I haven't had anything to eat for two days."

"What happened?" I enquired.

"I had to stay at the hospital to attend to Tione. You know she's been admitted with malaria."

"Yes. I was meaning to visit her yesterday when all this happened. I didn't have time. How is she?"

"Picking up, but very slowly. She throws up everything she takes. If only she could eat. Did you have anything to eat this morning?"

"Oh, yes!" Pilira chuckled. "I didn't want what happened in Lambulira to happen to me again."

She was referring to the funeral of my eldest brother's son. I had given them the bus fare to go on the previous day. They had arrived in the evening, slept without supper, got up, no one had given them breakfast. There had been no lunch, either. I had given them a lift home in the afternoon. Luckily, I had brought some bread and roast meat with me for such emergencies. They, or rather we, had devoured everything in the car. Including the raw peanuts, but not quite all. Pilira had taken some of the peanuts home. For planting, she said. There was a patch she hadn't got seeds for. I had not said anything.

We munched the bananas and stopped in Luchenza to wash them down with soft drinks. Of course, I paid for the round.

The Mulanje Massif reared its head higher and higher as we drove into the outskirts of the town. Several times I resisted stopping to take a photo of this, the highest mountain in the country. I had my multi-purpose Japanese camera in the boot.

"It's kind of hazy to take good pictures," Ndilipo commented.

I agree, since I'm still something of an amateur. "It's just that I might not be coming this way again for some time."

The impulse was almost irresistible as we neared the village. The mountain was so near, so clear, so overwhelming—you could see the blue-gray veins flecked with the white of falling water. Yet being so near the funeral, I did not have the heart to indulge in such an irreverent act. It would feel as if I was taking pictures of the corpse itself.

We turned the corner of the village track and hit a wall of wailing as they saw us. I came to a halt, and again the lump in my throat crept up, threatening to explode, as the women in my car burst my eardrums joining in the lamentations.

> *My sister! My sister!*
> *Who shall I remain with*
> *Now that you're gone*
> *Oh, mother! Oh, father!*

I got busy ostentatiously winding up windows and locking up doors, to allow all the emotions let loose around me to subside.

The women were led inside to where the body was. We men were led to a tree under which some chairs had been arranged in a rough semicircle. I noticed that on two *khonde*s there were other knots of men on chairs representing different groups. The one above us was the church officials. The one below was the village headmen. Our group—the relatives from Zomba, Blantyre, and Mulanje—were sandwiched between these two groups. We were introduced to both groups, all in good time.

We sat there under the tree, listening to the hymns coming from the church women with the body in the house. Hymn after hymn rebounding from the granite face of Mulanje, cascading back to us below. There were some wood shavings, offcuts, planks near the tree, so the coffin must have been made right under the mourners' noses.

"We've done everything as you ordered." This was addressed to ME! "Alinafe was here early in the morning and told us to go ahead with the coffin and the grave-digging. That you would sort everything out when you got here."

I expressed my apologies for coming late.

"We bought the planks from the forestry department. The carpenter has done a good job. We got a colorful cloth for the covering. It's all in place. We are now just waiting for the grave-diggers to tell us they've finished. The ceremony will start soon, now you're here with the Zomba people."

I sighed inwardly. Now, as usual, it was MY funeral. Now I had to shoulder all the responsibility for bringing all these people here, even the corpse, I supposed. One of these days, I agonized, I'll stop going to my relatives' funerals. Each time one of us dies, they all behave as if I'm the sole proprietor, and therefore chief financier, not mourner, of the funeral. Each funeral has a nightmarish similarity about it, whether in the villages at home or for relatives far from home: uncle, mother, cousin, aunt, nephew, or niece. Ever since my first job. More so since I had been transferred to my home district.

The grave-diggers sent word that their job was finished and the ceremony soon started. It began with the bereaved viewing the body. We trooped inside amid hymns and more wails, going round the coffin surrounded by the church women and coming out the way we had gone in.

There she was lying in the open coffin. Only the top half of her face was visible—the rest was covered with a blanket, not a cloth. She was almost hairless, tufts of brownish black hair sprouting sparsely on taut skin. Her skin had become lighter, too. There she was, the subject of my agonies.

What was she really to me? It wasn't as if she was even my sister. Only a cousin, really, with her own brothers. Where was the other? When I phoned him yesterday, he said he couldn't make it to Mulanje from Lilongwe in one day, if the burial was on Monday. I was to go ahead with it. He didn't even mention the expenses or how I was to get half the village to Mulanje in one small saloon.

My encounters with Zinenani had been very scattered, since I had grown up away from home. I had only come home occasionally during the holidays. When she had got married, she had gone away to live with her husband. It was only when she had been getting a divorce that I had been involved in the court case. I had been overruled when I had protested that I hadn't been present at the original officiation. I wasn't even a *nkhoswe* or witness to the marriage. Neither had I known her husband before, nor had I liked what I had seen of him later. I had to attend court, they had said. I had advised them to ask for a postponement and transfer to an urban, not a traditional, court that was speeding up the process of divorce. I had again been overruled. They had gone ahead. I had been irrelevant throughout, since I had not known the circumstances surrounding their marriage, nor the grounds for divorce, either. Zinenani had been granted less than K500, to be paid in installments. I learned later that not even one eighth of this had been paid. That had been why

Zinenani had started selling her possessions soon after and had not stopped until just before her death.

She had also become insufferable once she had settled back in the village. Her caustic tongue, town airs, and drunken tendencies had made her more enemies than friends. Some of her relatives had stopped talking to her, let alone visiting her. I guess her fleeing to the hospital, and later to her uncle in Mulanje had been a premonition that she was not loved at home. If she had died at home, she would have been buried like a dog, with only a handful of people present. And here she was being given full Christian honors.

In actual fact, it was me who had taken her to the hospital the first time. I had gone to my nephew's funeral, and since I had not seen Zinenani at all for some time, after the ceremony I had stopped by. She had looked so deathly ill, I had asked Nankhoma what was happening and what they were doing to help her. Zinenani could hardly lift herself to eat. Her feet and stomach had swollen up so much they looked as if they would burst if you pricked them. I had told them to get her ready the following morning, when I would take her to the hospital. They had admitted her immediately.

I had asked for the diagnosis: Sclerosis of the liver. What could be done to help her? Nothing. In other countries, they could have tried an expensive transplant. Here, the clinical officer shrugged helplessly, nothing could be done. They could keep her in hospital, try to pump her with liquid nutrients which she would keep losing at the other end, for as long as the liver could hold out. Or the relatives could take her home to look after her themselves. The hospital was already overcrowded, as I could see, two to a bed and some more on the floor.

I had gone to Nankhoma and the relatives again. Yes, they would look after her. I had brought her home and the next thing I heard, she had gone to Mulanje.

It had not been an easy trip, I was told later. She had walked three kilometers to catch a bus to Blantyre at a roadside stop. In Mulanje, she had got lost and collapsed under the trees of a tea estate. A good Samaritan had come across her in that condition, asked her where she was going. He had lifted her onto his bicycle carrier and brought her to her uncle after several rests on the way. That had been Thursday. No one had known about her, because Mwatitha had come to Zomba that same day to visit her. They had missed each other on the way. He had got the message on Friday that she had arrived in Mulanje. He had got back to Mulanje on Saturday. It was sheer desperation, what with two other patients already under his roof, that had made him ask for my help from Zomba.

YOU KILLED HER, the accusation jolted me out of my complacency since yesterday, as soon as Alinafe told me in the second phone call that Zinenani had died. There was I, eating stewed chicken with boiled potatoes and turnip greens, thinking of the nap afterwards, while Zinenani was in her death throes. All I could think of was how tired I was after two trips to Blantyre on two successive days. Zinenani had had two bus trips on a sick liver which had made her collapse in the white man's tea estate, where a complete stranger had taken pity on her. And all I could accuse her of was her irresponsible behavior. Sick people should not behave like that. Have I ever been so hopelessly sick as to know what goes on in the minds of people close to death? Who am I to talk about irresponsibility?

"… *Howl, ye inhabitants of the isle* …"

The preacher's voice clamored in my ears. It felt like the flapping of an owl's wings beating the meaning of the words into my conscience.

The reading was from the prophet Isaiah, warning this tiny island people that, when their destruction was near, they should not clamber into their own boats to escape. The boats had already been sabotaged by their enemy. They should shout so that the untampered mainland boats could come and save them. Here were Zinenani and Mwatitha shouting from Mulanje over the telephone wires for me to come all the way from Zomba to help them. Their own boats or means of escape were inadequate, they were dying. I heard their desperate shouts and did not speed to their rescue.

COME OFF IT. WAKE UP. YOU'VE GOT IT ALL WRONG. Something came over me again. All the while the church elder was reading and the reverend later interpreting, I had been wondering how the reverend could connect this irrelevant prophecy to the realities of

Zinenani's funeral—markets, island cities, boats, sabotage, and the mainland had nothing to do with these grass-thatched, mud-walled huts under the glowering Mulanje Massif. Then the preacher's eyes, hands, gestures looked to the sky glowing beyond Mulanje Mountain.

"The boat," he shouted to Sapitwa Peak, pointing with open arms, palms upward, "is coming from Jesus. Jesus is the boat, brothers and sisters. Unless we call for Jesus' boat, we shall all sink."

I heaved a sign of relief: Zinenani had not been shouting for me. Mwatitha had not been calling for my car to bring Zinenani to safety in Zomba. ZINENANI HAD CALLED FOR THE BOAT OF JESUS IN MULANJE, AND IT HAD COME TO HER IN ALL ITS GLORY. In Zomba, no churchmen or women would have sung or preached at her death. In Mulanje, the reverend in his white collar and black cassock stood resplendent over the elders, the church women, around Zinenani's boat that was her coffin. SHE WAS ON HER WAY TO CHRISTIAN SALVATION—WAS ALREADY THERE.

Suddenly, all that I had done seemed trivial. All that was happening round Zinenani's coffin gathered deeper significance. How petty we are in our small concerns! Even Zinenani's arrogance and caustic tongue seemed to be charged with the single-mindedness of a religious fanatic. All we had been doing was to stop her from getting onto that boat. We had been obstacles to her salvation, as she disdainfully brushed us away from the path chosen for her.

As we trudged to the graveyard, my heart was heavy. I didn't walk beside any of my relatives, although they were all around me, some of them actually swapping jokes and laughing, some arguing about the existence of the soul after death.

"I've never heard of a bank of spirits," said Atani, my Blantyre brother, "somewhere up there."

Fatsani shushed him.

"Have you ever heard those people who come from the dead talk?"

"One of these days," Fatsani said in subdued tones. "We should sit down and argue these things out."

"Sure," Atani was irrepressible. "If you tell me what Lazarus said to his relatives after coming back to life, I'll believe you."

He sounded almost like my drowned uncle. I didn't want to get involved. We turned into the graveyard, and trudged all the way over to the corner, where a high mound of freshly dug soil sat.

When the grave ceremony finished, the relatives hung behind as if by common consent.

'This is where Aunt Ndakulapa lies, and this is where Cousin Ndayesa is buried." Uncle Mwatitha went from tomb to tomb almost proudly.

"Zinenani now lies here, surrounded by all these relatives who have gone before her. It is their call she came to answer. For this they are grateful, and have received her wherever they are."

I quivered inside as we trooped out of the graveyard to follow fellow celebrants and mourners.

"That's Sapitwa Peak." Uncle Mwatitha pointed to Mulanje Mountain again as we walked back.

"What's so famous about it?"

"That is the abode of the Great Spirit. All the spirits congregate there to form one Great Spirit. Even the white men coming all the way from America or Europe to climb the mountain are really invited by the spirits. When the mountain climbers have disappeared, they have gone to join the Great Spirit. You spend weeks or months on foot or in a helicopter looking for them. You won't find them. How can you find a spirit?"

I looked around for Atani. He was gaping fearfully at the massif in front of us.

Most of the helpers were eating or had eaten by the time we joined them at the village. Platefuls of *nsima* and fish were brought to the different groups—chiefs, relatives, and churchmen—to eat. Our group did not have the heart to eat. The food was taken away again, after our refusal, for the other groups to eat. I confess my mouth was dry, my stomach was empty, I yearned for something to eat, but could not bring myself to get up and go inside to eat.

Instead, we turned now to the funeral expenses.

"We bought the planks ...," Mwatitha began.

It was an anticlimactic travesty, so I asked him just to give us the total they had spent. Between us we contributed to half the sum. I had to top it up, of course, as usual, so that Mwatitha owed no one for Zinenani's funeral afterwards.

***

"You should start with us," Alinafe implored. "Just drop us at the bus station. We'll take the bus from there. You can then come back to collect the Zomba group you came with."

There was no other car left and it was almost two kilometers to Mulanje *boma*. It was already something to five. If they were to catch the last bus, they needed to be there now. I rearranged my itinerary again. Alinafe had brought Fatsani and two elderly women from Limbe. They bundled into the car.

"The last bus has already gone," we were told at the station.

"We'd better try the shopping centre for *matola*."

We found a small truck already full to the brim.

"We're only going as far as Thyolo."

"That's all right. We'll catch a minibus from there."

"Could you give me money for transport for the women?" Alinafe turned to me.

"What?!"

"They're my friends, and they came without any money. And they did help us bury Zinenani, you know."

I fished out some paper money, speechless. As I drove back to Mwatitha's village, I fumbled in the carton under the front seat. I found a small plastic bag and pulled it out. It was full of roast chicken. I selected a thigh and started munching. This was my lunch for the day. My mouth was watering and I couldn't chew fast enough. I had finished the thigh by the time the Zomba group met me and piled inside. I turned and drove back to the main road.

"So you had some chicken this time." Ndilipo had found the plastic bag. "We shouldn't give any to the women."

"Why not?"

"They've already eaten. While we were busy talking finances."

Actually, he had not contributed anything himself. No money, he'd said.

168

"We're still hungry." A voice came for the back.

I passed the bag over.

"Don't finish it," Ndilipo looked over his shoulder, worried. "Actually, it's pork I miss most."

"I've got some pork, too, but I don't want you to touch it."

"We have pork in Santhe, but I have no money to buy it."

The same litany. Everywhere I go. I reached for the carrot bag. Ndilipo reached for the dinner rolls in another bag.

We stopped at a hotel in Limbe for drinks. It was almost seven by then.

"We can't go into the lounge like this." The women looked at their *zitenje*, soiled feet, and uncombed hair tied crudely in small head scarves.

We trooped onto the *khonde*, pulled more chairs up around a table. Some curious faces turned to stare at us. I ignored them and called for a waiter. I ordered mine and went to the gents. That's what I needed most. That's why I had stopped there, in fact.

"Next time, you should buy me a bottle of wine," said Pilira when I rejoined the group.

"You should have ordered it when you had the chance," I told her.

"That's what I told her," Ndilipo said, "when you were away."

"I was afraid."

"Thank goodness! You have no idea how much a bottle of wine costs!"

"Let's go!"

I paid the bill and followed them out to the car. The street lights were on now. I turned on the car radio. A listener's request was on—a local number:

> *Tell me, mother,*
> *I want to get married*
> *But the men don't want me*
> *Oh dear, Oh dear*
> *What wrong did I do, mother?*
> *I also wash with soap.*
> *I dye my hair.*
> *I apply oil on my skin.*

"Exactly," Pilira interrupted. "That's what I wanted to tell you."

"Me?" I was startled.

"Yes, Limbanazo. You come to the village and you never even look at me. When you do, it's as if you were looking at sweepings."

She was my eldest brother's age. In fact, if Atani had not grown up away from the village, they would have been made to marry. Why she picked on me I don't know.

"Why don't you get married, then."

"Why should I get married to someone who can't afford to buy soap, like me?"

"There's Ndilipo here."

"Him? He's already finished."

"Look," I said, "here is the pork I was talking about."

"We never see these things in the village."

"Maybe," I said grimly, "you should go more often with me to funerals. Do you know that what you've eaten in this car would have cost us more than K200 at the hotel?"

I dropped Ndilipo in Santhe. On his doorstep, in fact. The problem was the women. I couldn't let them sleep in town—there were too many of them and they had already drained all my resources, not to mention my emotions. Dropping them in the village meant negotiating a bumpy, rocky, gullied dirt track two kilometers long. Each time I go over it I have to take the car to the garage to have the undercarriage or engine mounting repaired, or the exhaust pipe welded, or suchlike. That's one of the reasons I don't go to the village too often. The car bills are not amusing.

"You don't mind," I asked as we sped through Zomba town center, "If I drop you off at the turn-off by the roadside? I can't go on that road in the dark."

"We can't walk in the dark like this, either," Pilira protested. "Two women all alone with a baby."

"There are thugs on that road," Nankhoma joined in. "They wait for drunkards from the bars, bottle stores, and taverns to come up there at night."

They helped bury Zinenani, you know, Alinafe's words about her Limbe friends came back to me. This was the Zomba troop of mourners the Mulanje people had been waiting for. I turned into the dirt track that led to my mother's village. The same one I had taken yesterday—it seemed ages ago—to tell them of Zinenani's demise.

True enough, there were two thugs standing just off the road near the stony place I had to negotiate at zero kilometers per hour. The full beam caught them were. I thought they were going to jump on the car, since I was driving so slowly they could have smashed it with the rocks lying all around. However, they went on talking to each other, as if discussing which part of the garden they should start clearing the following morning. By the time we passed them, the fan was working to cool the engine. I sped dangerously over the bumpy patches, just to keep the air circulating faster to stop the fan. I had to slow down again half a kilometer beyond, to go over another rocky place. And a small gully after that, before we got to our village.

"They know the mourners are back," Pilira said unnecessarily as the full beam cut the pitch dark for all the world to see in front of us. The little tin paraffin lamps in the windowless huts around us could not illuminate the outside at all.

"Here we are."

"I can't believe we've been to Mulanje and back all in one day. Thank you very much."

I didn't want to tell her I could have made it in fewer hours really, in spite of the stopovers.

"Now, Limbanazo," she had the last word, "don't forget what I told you about soap and marriage. We mature women these days want young men like you."

"Goodnight." I started the engine. If I ever wanted polygamy, it would certainly not be with Pilira.

I heard the sound of wailing above the engine as I coasted back down. I did not stop to investigate; probably an out-of-towner had come home believing the burial would be in Zomba. Well, someone else could sort that out.

"Look!" Thokozani pointed to a figure in the dark.

I slowed down to negotiate the rocks again and saw the third thug. The newcomer, although much younger than the others, looked infinitely more ferocious. I hope I don't have reason to walk up or down the road at night.

It was an uneventful trip to and from Likale to drop Thokozani, the last passenger. But morbid thoughts kept looming over the horizon of my consciousness: was Masautso, after all his minor operations, going to die too? Or Tione, with malaria? I could not get them out of my mind.

"How did it go?" my wife greeted me as I got home.

How does one describe a funeral? It went fine or badly? I was at a loss as to what to say.

"She had a decent burial," I summed it up slowly. "More than she could have had at home."

The Hyena Wears Darkness

1

Ndamo, seated on his grass *khonde*, gave Agogo's hut across the *kapinga* grass another questioning glance. He had been doing so since the sun's rays pierced through the mango tree leaves towering over his house. The furrows between his gray eyebrows deepened at each glance. Although it was understood that Ndakulapa would sleep with the widow for the *kusudzula*, the participants were expected to still wake up at a decent time. Now, with the mango tree shadow retreating from the front yard of the bereaved's house, even the children would know Ndakulapa was Atupele's *fisi*, hyena for the widow's cleansing ceremony. Such public knowledge of a supposedly secret rite would only get Ndamo into trouble again with the government projects people.

"Don't you think you should wake them up now?" Perturbation rasped Ndamo's voice as he asked Pumulani, his wife, bustling around in the outhouse they used as a kitchen.

"You should be the one to do it." Pumulani emerged squinting at him in the searing sunlight. She was a thin angular woman with *nchoma* tattoos on both cheeks. She had a *biriwita* wrapper tied with a cloth belt around the waist.

"I can't do it." He declined the invitation. "Atupele is my daughter-in-law."

"So is she mine," she said pointedly, shaking her head.

They both directed their gaze across the intervening grass expanse to Agogo's hut.

"This is a distressing business," Ndamo declared. "How can they embarrass us like this? Where is Atupele's mother?"

"Having breakfast in the kitchen." Pumulani unrolled the mat she had left on the *khonde* and sat on it. "She said she's leaving as soon as she's finished. You didn't expect her to go over there, did you?"

"Who else will do it?" He waived his arms around. When he was trying to contain his thoughts or emotions he pulled his mouth muscles

173

back, at the same time puffing his cheeks. "The kids shouldn't be involved in this."

"Even if it's her daughter in there," Pumulani pointed out, "Andaunire is our visitor here."

"I will do it then." Ndamo ground his teeth, pulling back his closed lips. "Even though Ndakulapa is my nephew, he is supposed to report to us."

Ndamo made a show of getting up from the cane chair, then going down the steps of the *khonde* on to the grass. He smarted at being corrected by his wife on a point of protocol. He was also full of misgivings about permitting the cleansing ceremony to go ahead when he was on the project's village committee. The project's people, together with the village committee members at several workshops, had identified traditional customs deemed hazardous to health. *Kusudzula*, the widow's sexual cleansing, *kuchotsa fumbi*, the deflowering of initiates, and *kulowa kufa*, wife inheritance, were clearly at the top of the risk list. And here he was supervising *kusudzula* right after Pangapatha, his son, was buried yesterday.

The door to Agogo's hut squeaked open. Ndamo, about to climb the single step up to it, checked and stepped aside. Atupele, the widow herself, emerged hesitantly, then slipped just outside the door. She wore the same blue spotted *chitenje* of yesterday with a blouse in a darker shade. As a sign of respect for the young woman, Ndamo sat on the *khonde* to one side of the doorway. Atupele shifted to the other side and knelt down. This positioning made it easier for both to converse without having to face each other directly. There was an awkward silence. Ndamo cleared his throat resolutely.

"You have slept well, my daughter?"

"Very well, father." Atupele sniffed.

A hesitant pause again, followed by another question: "Is my nephew still sleeping?" His head inclined in the direction from where she had surfaced.

"I slept alone." Atupele bowed her head.

"You what ...?" Ndamo jerked upright.

"He left last night …." Atupele averted her eyes. Her voice trailed off tremulously.

"Did he …?" Ndamo stopped himself; he couldn't throw such an intimate question at his own daughter-in-law. It would be another breach of protocol.

Atupele started sobbing quietly. Ndamo ground his teeth, perplexed. He was quite relieved to see Mrs Andaunire coming, closely followed by Pumulani.

"What is it, my daughter?" The two older women joined Atupele on the *khonde*, away from Ndamo.

"Don't start us crying again."

"My nephew didn't sleep in there," Ndamo volunteered when Andaunire's question was only received with heaving, shuddering sobs.

"Then where did he sleep?" Pumulani looked around.

"He couldn't have slept in the bereaved's house," Ndamo said.

"He wasn't supposed to. He doesn't know anybody around to have slept anywhere else."

"It's not a matter of where he slept," Ndamo snapped. "Where is he now? He can't be sleeping, wherever he is."

"He couldn't have gone home without bidding us farewell," Pumulani responded.

Ndamo turned to Atupele. "What happened last night?"

Atupele's sobs turned into full-throated wails. Ndamo quailed visibly. He wouldn't make any headway like this. As custom demanded, the older women joined in the lamentations. "Pangapatha! Iih!" "Who am I going to stay with, Pangapatha?" "Oh, my mother!" Ndamo simmered where he sat: soon the whole compound would be filled with more wailing women. Ndamo came to a decision. He stood up and signaled to Pumulani to follow him. He waited for her a short distance away. Pumulani came and knelt down in front of him.

"When Atupele has calmed down, find out what really happened last night. I will check on Ndakulapa from the *adzukulu* over there." He turned in the direction of the bereaved's house. He proceeded across the grass. The wailing women behind him reminded him of Pangapatha's funeral yesterday.

175

He had known Pangapatha was dying when he visited him in hospital at Kamba the week before. It was only a matter of how soon. The doctors couldn't tell him what was killing his son, but Ndamo had guessed. Some of his nephews and nieces had looked just as wasted and shrunk as Pangapatha before they finally died. Then three days ago Atupele brought her husband's body in Sigele Jika's pickup. There were no hitches till the question came up of which male relative would perform the cleansing ceremony with the widow.

Sigele Jika, being Ndamo's nephew and the deceased's brother, was the most likely candidate. Although very reluctant, he would have complied till Ndakulapa, the older brother, showed up. Sigele then conveniently abdicated his role to Ndakulapa, pointing out that the elder was the Jika family's *nkhoswe* in traditional transactions. The elders had assented to the switch of hyenas. Ndakulapa had then taken over the proceedings. But now it seemed as if Ndakulapa, too, had abdicated. Being a three-day ceremony, the rite was incomplete. Why had Ndakulapa accepted the role of hyena in the first place, then?

The bereaved's house was long emptied of ordinary mourners and sympathizers. Busy inside, though, were the *adzukulu* from the neighboring villages, who were responsible for preparing the body and the graveyard. What was remaining this morning was to mop the walls and floors of the bereaved's house with medicated water, to clear it of spirits and witches. Ndamo found the oldest one supervising in the next room.

"Did you see Ndakulapa here last night?"

"As you can see, we are only the *adzukulu* here. The rest have gone till the *kumeta*, shaving of hair, tomorrow."

"He couldn't have gone to Fikani." Ndamo retraced his steps but headed for his own house this time. Things seemed to have quietened down at Agogo's hut. Pumulani found Ndamo in his former place soon afterward. As before, she sat on the mat.

"He didn't sleep there either," Ndamo reported.

"This is the work of witchcraft," Pumulani opined. "It's unheard of to abandon the rite on the first night. Perhaps he didn't know that ...."

"It's not his first time, even in Mutopa," Ndamo cut her short.

Mutopa village was not so-named for nothing. It was the village mourning. In the past, the deaths were attributed to witchcraft. In recent years, it was because of what the villagers called "the government disease," AIDS, on account of the intervention from that quarter. The deaths had become regular, too. That was one of the reasons the government projects people had selected Mutopa for its pilot workshops on HIV/AIDS. The focus was on hazardous traditional practices. The elders' counterarguments were: with what were they to replace them, since they were well established? The projects people had advised: let's work together to find ways of turning these customs into positive weapons of change.

"We'll have a scandal on our hands." Pumulani wrung her hands. "We'll be the laughing stock of Mutopa. What will the people say when they hear that our hyena fled the ritual hut in the night?"

"We'll have a scandal of a different kind," Ndamo corrected. "What will the projects people say when they hear that our committee members consented to the ritual behind their backs? All the plans for the orphan care and skills center will be canceled now."

"Don't believe everything those people promise you. Mutopa will be as it was before they came."

"You don't know anything," Ndamo scoffed. "Look at Gawani village. They not only built a skills center there, they transformed the path into a road connecting it to the main one. They brought in water pumps. There's now talk of building a clinic there."

"Let them build those things there!" Pumulani brushed him aside. "Who are the projects people to tell us what to do in our own land? Without the cleansing ceremonies, we will have more deaths in Mutopa. Just imagine different groups of mourners passing each other twice on the same day, one from one burial, the other to the next."

"Those are the kinds of beliefs the projects people want to discourage. These cleansing ceremonies are the real cause of disease, they maintain."

"They are the kind of beliefs that sustained our forefathers," Pumulani put in impatiently. "We have been through this before, my husband. We didn't establish the customs ourselves, today or yesterday. We found them. We inherited them. They, too, inherited them from their forefathers, passed on from generation to generation. How can the projects people believe we can abandon our customs just because they'll build us a road to the *boma*?"

"What are we going to do now?" Ndamo cut her ramblings short.

"We have a crisis on our hands. The only thing that'll save us is to find your nephew and bring him back here!" Pumulani then grew more conspiratorial. "He's got to complete the ceremony. The young man did it only once and fled without explanation."

Ndamo's lips and cheeks grew very agitated. "But having fled from here, what will make him return and be laughed at?"

"You know the alternative is to hire a *namandwa*—the professional hyena—and start all over again."

"Those people cost a lot of money; we can't afford it."

"Exactly, and we want to keep the ceremony within the family. So it has to be your nephew. Which means today. The shaving of the hair is tomorrow. And Andaunire is breathing fire again. She is threatening to take us to court for breaking our part of the ceremony."

Andaunire had brought the appropriate medicines all the way from Mbamba, her lakeshore home. In fact, she was the one who had pressurized them to *sudzula* Atupele the night of her husband's burial.

"Do you know what this means?" Ndamo almost yelped. "I will have to catch a bus to Fikani and back."

"What else can we do? You're his uncle and the only one he will listen to."

"All for the sake of cleansing a widow?"

"You and I know that *kusudzula* is more than cleansing the widow. The union of man and woman brought us all into the world. We are severing the bond that tied the husband and wife together. You can't have a spirit tied to a living person. It will cause havoc for her and the whole community."

"This is a very depressing business." Ndamo pulled back his lips. "Here we are, wallowing between what the ancestors taught us to revere and what the tribe has to do to survive. Half of me says do what is right by your forefathers. The other says do what is right for your people, the ancestors will understand."

"You don't have only your forefathers to contend with. Right now Andaunire is coming to find out what you are going to do about her daughter."

"Tell her I'm on my way." Ndamo pulled himself together. He found Andaunire a formidable woman. He did not want another confrontation with her. He had consented to every suggestion she had made. It had resulted in shortening the period of the cleansing ceremony. She also had shortened the period she could stay after burial. She had declared she wasn't even going to stay for the *kumeta*. That was for Atupele, she said. I've a business to look after at Mbamba. Potential violence bubbled under her imposing frame. Each time she turned a baleful eye to him, he quivered inwardly. He caught the same expression on her face as she advanced purposefully towards his house.

"I have got to change." Ndamo got up precipitately. "I can't be taking buses and making visits in these tatters."

2

Ndakulapa didn't know whether to bellow like a wounded buffalo or whimper like a mongrel that had received a whack on its behind. He erupted from Agogo's hut, stumbled, and almost fell down the step that led him onto the level ground outside. The tropical night draped his form like a black shroud, as he got his bearings on the *kapinga* grass that separated Agogo's hut, the bereaved's house, and Uncle Ndamo's. He couldn't go into the bereaved's house to join other mourners on their second day of the wake. He certainly wasn't going back to Uncle Ndamo's house. He wasn't expected to report on how the *kusudzula* ceremony had gone with Atupele, the widow. He just couldn't face anyone after what had happened in Agogo's hut that night or even the morning after. In the end, he slunk away from Mutopa like a marauding hyena that had been thwarted of its prey.

It wasn't that Uncle Ndamo and the elders weren't expecting an immediate report. It was that Atupele had given a medical report he wasn't prepared to present to anyone, now or perhaps ever. There was a devastating message involved.

"I am HIV positive," she had announced, soon after their sexual cleansing session. She said she was only returning the compliments to the family that had produced Pangapatha, who had infected her in the first place. Ritual or no ritual, how does one infected *fisi* report a message like that?

He had trembled where he stood, his bones shook inside him, and his manhood shrank between his legs. He wanted to scream, whimper, groan, or roar, but only the enormity of the news grew in the darkness confronting him. He even started hearing the funeral songs that had been sung that afternoon escorting Pangapatha, the widow's husband and his own cousin. They were now being sung for him.

Confused by this turn of events, Ndakulapa caught the late bus home. In transit, he swung between volcanic shudders and simpering sighs that made the other passengers shrink away from him fearfully. This turbulent state fueled him for the whole trip to Fikani village. It was almost midnight when Nansani, his wife, opened the door. She was clad in a *chitenje* only.

"What is it, father of Mwaona?" Nansani asked. She had lit a paraffin lamp before opening the door. She wasn't too sleepy to notice the murderous mood he was in. Ndakulapa brushed past her and slumped onto a chair. He cupped one fist in the palm of the other hand and pushed. The knuckles cracked rapidly one after another: *krr! krr! krr!*. He switched round and cracked the knuckles of the other hand. *Krr! krr! krr!* ricocheted in the room. He breathed noisily.

"How did the funeral go?" Nansani asked hesitantly from another chair round the small table meant for four people.

"Don't ask stupid questions. How do funerals go: fine or badly?"

Ndakulapa's roar seemed to fling Nansani backward in her chair. When she recovered slightly she ventured again. "Shall I cook something for you? I wasn't expecting you tonight, so I didn't keep …."

"When were you expecting me? Just go back to bed, woman." Nansani fled. A doorless wooden frame separated her from her husband's wrath. She sat on the mat beside the single bed that was the only furniture. She cowered in the dark, wondering what was coming next.

In the front room, Ndakulapa leaned his elbows on top of the small table. The fists which now supported his forehead closed his eyes, they hurt. He remained in that position, reviewing the events of the past twelve hours.

Ndakulapa got the news of Pangapatha's death just yesterday morning. He boarded a bus for Njati soon afterward, to be in time for the burial. Sigele Jika, his younger brother, was already at Mutopa, having transported the corpse and the widow there. In fact, Ndakulapa could trace his present predicament to Sigele and his refusal to be the relative-on-the-spot for the widow's *kusudzula*. At the last moment, Sigele had abdicated his appointment, pointing out that it was Ndakulapa's duty to fulfill the hyena's role, now that he was present, since he was the Jika family's *nkhoswe*. The elders assented. Ndakulapa met his nemesis that way.

Ndakulapa's mind seethed with all the options before him. Now that he was infected, should he tell his wife the truth? If he didn't tell her, would he infect her, too? If he kept quiet but did not fulfill his conjugal obligations, what explanation would he give her? How long could he keep away from her before she started questioning or even importuning? He had told Atupele that Nansani was also steeped in traditional customs, but did his wife actually know that he was a hyena?

Unlike others, one didn't advertise the hyena profession. Although the elders appointed him because of his manifest prowess to begin with, they, too, did not declare publicly who was on their staff list. Hyenas, wearing the mantle of darkness, worked quietly, routinely cleansing their community of their iniquities. The coming of AIDS now threw the hyena practice into terrible disarray. Before it, they could go to the clinical officer or the medicine man for the smaller diseases. They got cured and continued their trade, their wives were none the wiser. But AIDS spelt sure death.

Ndakulapa had seen Nkalawire, his niece, break into spots and then develop a terrible cough. Thereafter they had watched her waste away and shrink under their very eyes. In the end, the once robust woman weighed no more than a little girl. Nkalawire was not the only case. Fikani had come to routinely bury their dead; they knew who suffered from the government disease, but even though alive, the patients tried to hide their status.

But then if one refused to perform the rites, there were always the *namandwa*, those professional ritual cleansers the people could turn to. So what was one to do now? Perhaps if he consulted Atsalaachaje, their local medicine man, right away, he could do it. Atsalaachaje was no mean choice. He plied his trade with the village and town. After his initial successes in Fikani and the neighboring villages, he had opened some clinics in Kamba city's townships. He specialized not only in bodily ailments, but also vanities: success in love, business, and the workplace. His regular customers were executives, managers, directors, shop-owners, contractors, and the like. Ndakulapa was a regular customer, to keep his tools of the trade always in working order.

Ndakulapa removed the knuckles from his closed eyes. The release of pressure hurt him as well. He sighed deeply and roused himself from the chair. Yes, he must go to Atsalaachaje before it was too late. He joined his wife in the next room as the second cock crowed.

The following morning found Ndakulapa saying the customary "Odi" in Atsalaachaje's front yard. Unlike others, the grass fence that enclosed his compound started in the middle of both sides of the main house. The fence itself had side doors that served as both entrances and exits. Atsalaachaje used the sitting room as the consultation room. This arrangement proved awkward when other patients were present. If you needed more private ministrations you made a special request. The man then took you outside to one corner of the house. Ndakulapa knew the routine and did not waste time with the preambles.

"Hyenas like you need protective medicine not only *nkhondokubedi* potency potions." Atsalaachaje was quite forthright with his patient. He wore ordinary clothes: a short-sleeved shirt; a pair of khaki trousers and sandals. He was as old as Ndamo but with darker and drier skin stretched over aged limbs.

"Do you have anything for this government disease?"

"If I was another kind of medicine man I would have given you an easy antidote going around these days."

"What's that?"

"It's like a cleansing ritual to get rid of the infection."

"What's done?"

182

"You sleep with your own daughter or niece. They have to be yours, of course, preferably virgins, too."

"I couldn't possibly do that."

"Come on, it's like *kuchotsa fumbi* and you have done it before. It's part of your work. In the night, you don't know who you're deflowering: a daughter, a niece, or someone unrelated to you. They all open their legs without declaring their names. You leave as anonymously as you came. No one knows it's you, their father, or uncle, during the day.

"But in this case I'd be known."

"I am not prescribing you that. I doubt if it works at all. It's just a license for incest if you ask me."

"Then do you have anything that works?" Ndakulapa implored, "because if you don't, this spells the death of hyenas. No hyena will continue working anymore in the face of AIDS."

"Frankly, my friend, we have no cure for it. Don't let anyone fool you on this. At first, we thought AIDS was *magawagawa*. So we treated it as such. Too late, we realized it wasn't, and we had no traditional answers for it. So we changed tactics. The same government that gave us AIDS brought ARVs. So what we do is to mix the *magawagawa* potions with the ARVs. It gives our patients more confidence that way. At least, they live longer than they would if they didn't take the concoction."

"Do you have them?"

"You don't have to get them from me. You would only have to pay me, when they are free in any government clinic."

"But that means being tested first, doesn't it?"

"Of course, they don't just hand them out like aspirin, you know."

"But for your patients it's a mixed formula, not so?"

"They are the ones who insist on it. They believe the old mixed with the new will cure them definitely. I comply; give the customer what he believes in. That's halfway toward curing him."

"Give me the mixed stuff, then. I've got to have it now while the virus doesn't know what to do with me. If I wait for testing at the clinic it will have settled in its new home."

"You see?" Atsalaachaje laughed. "You are the one insisting on the modified formula."

Atsalaachaje left Ndakulapa to go inside. He returned with a jugful of some liquid and a packet. "Take this now," he said with a smile, "since you are so desperate. The rest you take as prescribed at the clinics."

Ndakulapa took the first gulp and nearly choked. Atsalaachaje laughed. He watched his patient grimace and with grim determination drink the rest down.

"Have you heard of the *nansanganya?*" Atsalaachaje asked, retrieving his jug.

Ndakulapa's face was still twitching with distaste. "Is that it?"

"No. *Nansanganya* is the stuff the chiefs are using now for *kusudzula* and a few other rites."

"How can they do that? *Nansanganya* is only used for young initiates to protect them for the outdooring."

"Exactly. It has now been adapted to protect you fellows and widows from infectious diseases."

"What is the world coming to? Do these chiefs have proper *anamkungwi?* The man's and woman's fluids must mingle and go to the bones. When the man withdraws he draws out all her iniquities, too. That's what our forefathers told us."

"The chiefs are accepting the new modified version to protect their people. A chief is a chief because he protects his people, that is, living people. The people are dying with our *kusudzula*, *kuchotsa fumbi*, and *kulowa kufa* because that's where they are getting the AIDS from, like you have done. What does it profit a chief if he rules an empty village? Given the choice of death or adaptation the chiefs have opted for life."

"They must be progressive chiefs, then."

"They are. These things are happening now all around you. I'm now making quite a lot of business with *nansanganya*. I'm telling you this as one of my regular customers. Now that this thing has happened to you, I would think seriously about it. Talk to your relatives about it. You don't want them wiped out, too, because of you and your profession."

Ndakulapa left Atsalaachaje in as confused a state as he had come earlier. He reached home not knowing what to do next. He took the grass entrance to the back of his house. He shivered violently as if he had malaria when he saw Uncle Ndamo waiting for him on the *khonde*.

The Hyena Wears Darkness

3

Ndamo arrived at Fikani village just before noon. He wore a gray shirt and faded black trousers. Light brown socks and brown shoes covered his feet. He had taken time to comb his sparse gray hair, too. The slight frown still sat between his brows. He was perched on a chair on the *khonde*.

After the preliminaries of greeting a surprised Nansani, he was given boiled sweet potatoes to be washed down with black tea. They didn't talk much after. Nansani busied herself in the outhouse. Once she went out of the grass fence with a bucket. She apologized profusely for leaving the visitor alone. She came back with water. There were no children around. Ndamo was left to his own devices while waiting for his nephew. From his elevated position he had a view of the outhouses and bath-shed, enclosed by the grass fence surrounding the back of the house. Through the entrance of the fence, he could see a *nandolo* and maize garden. It was from the path alongside this garden that he saw Ndakulapa approaching.

Ndakulapa always reminded his uncle of grinding stones with the *mwanamphero* mate perched on top of it. Ndakulapa was of medium height with a small round head on top of disproportionately broad shoulders linked by a short neck. Ndamo quickly reviewed Ndakulapa's bewildering behavior the past few hours. It was so unprecedented the forefathers had not laid down what course of action to take should it occur. Ndamo stood up and went down the step. It was a considerably agitated nephew he now met.

"Uncle Ndamo," Ndakulapa said in a shaky voice. They shook hands, then Ndakulapa hastily disengaged himself. He turned and lifted the chair from the *khonde* to set it on level ground beside where Ndamo stood uncertainly.

"Sit down here. I will sit there." Ndakulapa sat himself on the bare *khonde* floor. Ndamo, after hesitating briefly, sat down again. Ndakulapa seemed to be struggling with a multitude of horrors threatening to tear his insides apart. Ndamo, on the other hand, looking like a living question, barely suppressed himself.

"You have traveled well, uncle?" Ndakulapa finally controlled himself to a communicable level.

185

"As safely as the bus driver allowed us to arrive in one piece." Ndamo looked at the other critically. "I see you arrived well, too."

Ndakulapa shifted uneasily where he sat, his face muscles working. He put his elbows on his thighs and passed his palm flat against his face as if to wipe out some terrifying vision. Then he pushed both palms to the sides of his face and hooked the thumbs behind the ears. He inhaled audibly.

"I must have left tracks of shame for you to find me so soon … so early, I was going to say."

"Only an incomplete job," Ndamo said simply. "There was only one place you could come back to."

"You find me in my hour of shame, having abandoned the widow."

"There is a lot we have got to discuss, my son," he puffed his cheeks by pulling his closed lips back.

"You sent me to my death," Ndakulapa whispered, shuddering.

"What are you talking about?" Ndamo leaned forward.

"The woman you gave me is death." Ndakulapa straightened his arms and held them clasped between his thighs. Then he stood up. "I left last night without bidding farewell to anyone to avoid another death."

"What death?" Ndamo's forehead knitted.

"Actually killing!" He clenched his fists. "I'd have strangled that woman."

"Atupele? Why?"

"She succeeded in killing me." An almost deranged laugh came out as Ndakulapa held his forehead helplessly.

"Can you please explain clearly what you're trying to tell me?" Ndamo stood and clasped his nephew's shoulder.

"The grave where I am going to be buried has already been measured and laid out for me. It is only waiting for the diggers to start their job. Each day, they'll call out for me to come and enter the hole, so they can go and rest. Each day, they'll wait for the walking corpse to come to his grave. My days are numbered. Atupele infected me with HIV. Soon I'll have AIDS and follow Pangapatha.." Ndakualapa sat down heavily.

Ndamo sat down too, suddenly. "It can't be. How do you know?"

"She told me herself, afterward of course."

186

"You mean Pangapatha died of AIDS?"

"Don't pretend you didn't know," Ndakulapa snarled. "You and the elders knew it but you sent me to her. I wasn't even supposed to be the hyena on this death. Sigele knew it and bolted. You all conspired to kill me through that woman."

"You are the *nkhoswe* of the family and there was no way we could've known …"

"Don't lie to me, otherwise I will really kill someone to accompany me to the grave."

Ndamo was too stunned to talk. Ndakulapa went on furiously.

"You visited your son in hospital. The doctors must have told you what was wrong with him."

Rather than risk another 'shut up,' Ndamo only shook his head. Ndakulapa went on relentlessly.

"The *adzukulu* prepared the body under your supervision. You lied to the church elders. You lied to the people. You lied …"

Ndakulapa shook where he sat. Ndamo cowered in his chair.

"This is a sorry business." His cheeks twitched up and down. "I was sent to bring you back."

"The only reason I will go back is to kill that witch," he hissed savagely.

"Stop blaming Atupele. My daughter-in-law is really a much-abused woman. Just imagine her husband dying on her. And there we were inflicting a strange man on her, on top of her tragic loss. How do you think all this affected her?"

"Should I feel remorse after what she did to me deliberately?"

"Like you and me, Atupele was only a victim of a rite that's threatening to wipe us all out. The least we can do is to make amends and try to reconcile with her. And you are the key person in this matter."

"I am the key person to my own death," Ndakulapa raved. "I went to her with my eyes wide open. Ach! This ritual is killing us all: First Pangapatha, then me. Next will be my wife, too. I don't know who else after that."

"That's it!" Ndamo changed tactics. "This might be the ancestors telling us to stop the rite now."

"How could the ancestors establish the custom and then come round to tell us to stop it?"

"We need to understand what is happening to us," Ndamo said earnestly. "This is what the projects people have been telling us all along. Our ancestors didn't have AIDS to contend with. Now there is AIDS and it is killing their children. They are telling us it's time to stop all this. Or as the projects people are saying, if that's difficult, to at least modify some of the customs before they destroy us."

"What do you mean?" Ndakulapa remembered Atsalaachaje's remarks earlier.

"At the last meeting of the council of elders we agreed to modify *kusudzula* by having the hyena and the widow go through a symbolic act of cleansing. There could be no direct contact."

"Then why did you let me go through the real method?" Ndakulapa asked wrathfully.

"Pangapathu died soon after the meeting," Ndamo told him hastily. "He had to be buried. Mrs Andaunire came with her medicines and pressured me to go on with the old hyena business. Everything happened so fast I was going to announce the modified method tomorrow at the *kumeta* ceremony."

"It's too late for me now. I am already infected. I am caught between the old and new methods. Either way I am dying."

"Not really," Ndamo shook his head vehemently. "The projects people have what they call ARVs. These are medicines for infected people, they say. If they can't cure AIDS, they at least give you long life. With them and at your age, you'll live your natural life span."

"This is what Atsalaachaje was trying to tell me."

"Who is Atsalaachaje?"

Ndakulapa explained, between shudders and deep exhalations. When he had finished, Ndamo got him by the shoulders again.

"You see?" he pointed out excitedly. "It's happening everywhere, even here. We were slow to catch on in Mutopa."

"What you are trying to tell me," Ndakulapa said wearily "is that you and the elders have already been convinced to abolish the custom that sustained our ancestors?"

"Not to abolish, but to modify them."

"Abolish or modify, what difference does it make? They are still being changed. This is a betrayal of the people by our trusted chiefs, headmen, and elders. You sold us to the projects people. We are defeated without even striking a blow. You, our elders, are now at the forefront, persuading us and supervising how to change our customs."

"Exactly, we need everyone to help us to protect our people. In this case, change is life. It is for the survival of the people. So will you please help, too?"

"In what way can I help you now?" Ndakulapa rasped indignantly. "You are propagating a symbolic method that needs no direct contact. To me, this spells my symbolic death. It is death to all hyenas."

"On the contrary, the hyenas continue their important role of cleansing the widow. They are crucial to the symbolic act. With this method, in the face of AIDS, we are saving both the widow and the hyenas. They survive to resume their ordinary roles as mothers and fathers in their own families."

"You know very well I did not apply for this job," Ndakulapa simmered: "You, the elders and my people, asked me to perform certain duties. You challenged us: where are our young men who can do this for us? Has their manhood been smashed falling from pawpaw trees? Has the hare run between their legs, rendering them impotent? Do we have to hire a *namandwa* to do the job for them? I answered the challenge and now look at me."

"Precisely. You are here because of the society's need for your services. Although you don't sit on the council of elders, you are a very, very important person to us. You are as important as the *adzukulu*, those people the same elders run to in times of bereavement to prepare the corpses and graveyards for us, since we can't do it ourselves. In fact, as you very well know, your cleansing job starts right after the *adzukulu* have finished theirs. What the people are asking you now, through me, is to continue your work as before."

"Even with this so called modified symbolic version?"

"Even because of it. The only difference is that you will now be working during the day and not concealed by darkness as before."

"It'll be a new kind of hyena, then," Ndakulapa pointed out ruefully. He reflected on the new role he had to play now. Being a successful hyena meant also being on good terms with the elders. They were the ones who assigned the duties. If they were modifying the customs, then their hyenas had to do the same. That was the only way to survive in the changed difficult circumstances. Even Atsalaachaje was modifying his concoctions.

"Yes," Ndamo assented, gravely, "one that can now sit side by side with the elders, openly involved in the affairs of the people. In fact, with your experience you can help us convert the people and the other hyenas by pointing out what you have been through. When you open your mouth you will be speaking from the depths of your heart. It will make the message more meaningful, credible and urgent."

"As you say or as your projects people say," Ndakulapa was pensive, "our ancestors didn't have AIDS confronting them. If they had had AIDS it'd have forced them to rethink their own traditions, too." He remembered Atupele's words last night: she said she, too, wanted to believe in the rite, but not when it was killing us all. They were now appealing to him to do something to rectify the situation. Ndakulapa was angry, but couldn't hang it on anyone in particular.

"We have been rethinking seriously about some of our customs after each workshop. We've come to realize more and more that we are all contributing to the mess we are in. In truth, veiled personal interests hide behind the stuff we claim to be customs. What is *kuchotsa fumbi* but man's license to be the first one to take the virgins before anyone else? What is *kusudzula* but coveting your brother's spouse, really? Some of this covetousness manifests itself in *kulowa kufa*, wife inheritance, which is a public declaration of polygamy. Just think of it, who stands to win in all this? Once you scrutinize these customs, all you see is man's lust, greed, and covetousness."

"But the women also consent to them." Ndakulapa re-examined his own work. He went over the amount of preparation he did on each assignment: including the potency potions, the anticipation of the performance with whoever happened to be the partner. Was that what custom demanded, what the society wanted of him, or was he fulfilling his own personal desires? Was it his own vested interests that had brought about his own infection?

"Out of fear," Ndamo cleared the mist, "confronted with the relatives' coercion, the widows submit."

"You sound more and more like Atsalaachaje."

"I would like to meet this medicine man of yours."

"I can take you to him before we return to Mutopa. In my new symbolic role of a daylight hyena, I will still need his *nansanganya*."

"He'll help us tremendously." Ndamo sighed, his mouth and cheeks working up and down.

Printed in the United States
by Baker & Taylor Publisher Services